DEVIL'S DOORSTEP

DEVIL'S DOORSTEP

PAUL EVAN LEHMAN

CUTTING EDGE

ISBN-13: 978-1-954840-01-0

Subsequently published as *Helltown*.

Published by
Cutting Edge Books
PO Box 8212
Calabasas, CA 91372
www.cuttingedgebooks.com

CHAPTER ONE

THE VERY MOMENT that he rode into the main street of Calder, Bill Borden knew that the fuse to some sort of explosion had been lighted and was sizzling.

To begin with, while the street was crowded there wasn't a single horse or vehicle at the hitching racks; secondly, the people seemed to be milling about rather than heading for any definite destination; and finally, the expression on the faces Bill saw was that of avid anticipation. The murmur of conversation reached him, but there were no undertones of jesting or laughter. Bill sensed that whatever was about to happen would be grim.

There were people on both sides of the street which stretched dusty and empty before him, and rather than make a one-man parade of himself Bill turned into a side street, followed it until he reached an alley paralleling the main drag, and rode along the alley to the center of town. There was a passageway between the Frontier saloon and a barbershop and he turned into it and halted his horse at the sidewalk. Here he would have an excellent view of whatever was about to happen. He shifted his weight in the saddle and set about rolling a cigarette, letting his gaze roam over the crowd on the far side of the street as he did so.

One figure caught his attention immediately. It was that of a tall, rawboned man with a mane of gray hair brushed straight back from a high forehead and hanging almost to his shoulders. His bony face was smooth-shaven and deeply lined, and the dark eyes beneath their bushy brows burned with the fire of a zealot. He wore black trousers, a black cutaway coat and a black string tie. A gambler? Bill thought not; those gnarled hands clenched into fists at his sides denoted power rather than skill and deftness.

Beside him, her hand clutching his arm, stood a girl. She was blonde, pretty and tranquil of feature, only her eyes betraying her emotion. They were large and deeply blue and at the moment appeared to be frightened. Bill guessed that this girl was the tall man's daughter.

He let his gaze travel on until it rested on another young woman. She was brunette, very trim and also pretty. Her expression was one of grimness rather than fear. She stood alone at the very edge of the street, and like the blonde young woman appeared out of place in this rough, raw town. Bill had heard Calder referred to as Hell's Back Yard and The Devil's Doorstep; he thought these two lovely young women better suited to stand at the gateway of Heaven.

In the rest of the crowd Bill saw only what he had expected to see in a town which was the haven for fugitives from the law. There were a few men who appeared to be tradespeople and a few women who might have been their wives or daughters. These were component parts of any Western frontier town. There were quite a number of flan-nel-shirted miners, a sprinkling of gamblers, a great many coarse-featured, well-heeled roughs, and a dozen or so slatternly women with the stamp of the honky-tonk upon them. These latter were not frightened either; they were merely excited and avidly curious.

A stir like that which galvanizes a crowd at the approach of a parade swept through the spectators. People ceased moving about and pushed to the edge of the street, all heads turned in the same direction. An almost inaudible whisper of "Here he comes!" ran along the sidewalks, and then, like an undulating wave, the ranks surged back to crowd against buildings and into doorways until, on the far side of the street, but three persons remained where they had originally stood. They were the tall, rawboned man, the blonde girl beside him and the young, neat and pretty brunette.

So it was to be a shooting affair, thought Bill. Such a thing was common enough in those days. Two men quarreled and an ultimatum was passed. "Get out of town or come a-shootin'." Bill leaned forward in the saddle and gazed interestedly in the direction the others were looking.

A man was approaching along the middle of the street. He was not a big man but there was confidence and fixity of purpose in his stride. He was dressed like a dude, with an enormous cream-colored Stetson hat, an ornate calfskin vest, whipcord trousers and black Spanish leather boots. His cartridge belt was hand-tooled and studded with silver, the holster was slung low and tied down, and the butt plates of his Colt were of mother-of-pearl. Bill wrinkled his nose in disdain; here was a gunman de luxe.

As though jerked by a hidden wire, heads turned to gaze in another direction, and Bill followed the tug of the string. Approaching from the other end of the street was a second man. He was a big man with a ruddy face and a huge mustache and calm, pale-blue eyes. He wore the garb of a cowman, plain and serviceable; his cartridge belt and holster were black and slick from use and his .44 had a plain walnut butt. He shuffled along the street pushing the dust away with his boots. This man, decided Bill, is a fighter but not a killer, with a confidence born of knowledge that his cause is a righteous one rather than the assurance that his draw is fast and his aim sure.

As this second contestant came abreast the Double Eagle saloon diagonally across the street from Bill, the swinging doors of the saloon parted and half a dozen cowboys emerged. They were keen-eyed and poker-faced as they moved along the plank sidewalk slightly to the rear of the one in the street, treading warily, spacing themselves so as not to get in each other's way. The big man saw them and turned his head and made an annoyed gesture, but they paid no attention to it. It was plain that they intended to see that he got a square deal whether he liked it or not.

The big man walked steadily, almost doggedly, and when he was fifty feet away Bill turned his head to watch the professional gunman. He was about the same distance on the other side of Bill, and Bill saw that he couldn't have picked a better place to view the conflict had he known in advance where the two would meet.

Both men continued to advance. The spectators were silent, pressing against the walls or crowded into doorways. Bill could see the faces of the more timid staring through window-panes from houses and stores.

The men were eighty feet apart—seventy—sixty. They slowed their pace slightly, becoming careful, wary.

The dark-haired girl stood at the edge of the street, every muscle tense, every nerve taut, her gaze fixed on the big man as though she would by some mental process add her strength and courage to that of his own. The tall, rawboned man opposite Bill gazed steadily at the approaching gunman as though to halt him by the very intensity of that stare. The blonde girl gripped his arm with both hands and dread in her eyes had grown.

They were fifty feet apart now; within the next ten feet—

The tall, rawboned man lifted a hand and gently disengaged the girl's fingers. He pushed her back, still gently, and stepped into the middle of the street, halting between the two men, facing the flashily dressed professional gunman. He raised his right hand, palm outward. Both men broke their remorseless strides and came to a halt.

The tall man spoke in a deep, impressive voice. "Thou shalt not kill. It is the Lord's commandment; it must be obeyed."

"A parson!" muttered Bill in astonishment. "A parson in Calder!"

The gunman spoke without moving his lips. "Get outa the way!"

"You and all the evil within you cannot move me, Smoke Rafferty!"

Coming from the lips of another it would have sounded melodramatic and stilted; coming from this man it was solemn, impressive. His voice grew in volume as he continued.

"The gold which the evil forces of this town would pay you for the murder of John Turner will not be earned. I am the Lord's representative in Calder, and I say you shall not kill him."

A shout came from somewhere in the crowd. "Stand aside, Parson, and we'll see which side the Lord's on!"

The preacher did not remove his intent gaze from the face of Smoke Rafferty. He said, "Blasphemy is one of the lesser sins of this evil town; we will concern ourselves with the greater ones first."

Rafferty, hoping to get a bead on Turner, side-stepped quickly, but the preacher moved with him. Rafferty whipped out his gun and arced it up to cover him, but the tall man did not falter.

Rafferty cursed. "Get outa the way or I'll drill you!"

The six cowboys who had been striding along the sidewalk had halted when the preacher had stepped into the street; now, at Rafferty's threat, six guns leaped from their holsters to cover the gunman. One of the cowboys said sharply, "You do, Smoke, and we'll blast you outa your fancy boots."

Bill Borden watched with narrowed eyes, his gaze moving swiftly from one actor in this drama to another. The cowman, John Turner, had halted some twenty-feet behind the parson; he stood with legs slightly spread and his body bent. He too had drawn his gun and he also waited to get in a shot. An equal distance in front of the preacher stood Smoke Rafferty, his face no longer imperturbable but white with anger. He had lowered his gun under the threat of cowboy Colts.

Bill glanced once more at the preacher standing like a monolith between the two men. Over the parson's head he caught a flutter of white from the sidewalk beyond. He saw a raised arm and a hand holding a handkerchief. The handkerchief moved slowly from side to side, then disappeared behind the heads of the spectators.

A shot boomed out.

Bill jerked his head to the right and upward. That shot had come from the roof of the Frontier saloon. He heard a strangled cry and looked back at John Turner. He was rocking on his heels; he had dropped his gun and his jaw sagged as though in consternation. He took a staggering step forward, then plunged face down in the dust.

There was an instant of horrified silence in which every movement was arrested; then came savage cries and people flooded into the street from both sides. The cowboys raised their guns and blasted away at the Frontier; the air stirred to the rush of leaden slugs which thudded into the false front or whined away into space.

Bill wheeled his horse and spurred him down the forty-foot passageway and into the alley. As he rounded the corner of the saloon he saw a horse standing close to the rear wall. Above the animal, suspended by hands which clung to the eaves, was a man. He let go and dropped into the saddle and the horse bounded away the instant he touched leather.

Bill spurred his mount and half a dozen great bounds brought him to the rump of the other's horse. The man flung a startled glance over his shoulder, then whipped out his Colt and twisted in the saddle. Bill slipped his right foot out of the stirrup, put his weight on the left and launched himself at the man as though about to wrestle down a steer.

His left hand gripped the fellow's six gun, the forefinger wedging itself between hammer and chamber; the other arm went about the fellow's waist. Gravity and momentum did the rest; the horses kept going but Bill's weight dragged the man from his saddle and they landed in the dust of the alley.

Bill still clung to the gun; he couldn't have let go had he wanted to, for the hammer, released, had driven the sharp firing pin deep into the flesh of his finger. He wrenched and the gun came free, still clinging to his hand. He was beneath the other, but a quick roll reversed their positions. He held himself tightly clamped to the killer, his face pressed against the man's chest, and the blows which the other struck landed feebly on his back.

There came a rush of feet and the six cowboys surged around the corner. Rough hands tore the two men apart and dragged them to their feet.

"Which one of you was it?" demanded their leader.

Bill said, "I caught him dropping off the roof. Nailed him when he hit the saddle."

A cowboy said, "That's straight, Wes. I seen this pilgrim setin' his hoss when John was shot. I seen him rein around and head back here. If it hadn't been for him this lousy killer woulda got away clean."

They released Bill immediately and turned their attention to the killer. He was a dirty, shifty-eyed man with fear written on his face. The one called Wes cursed him savagely and struck him on the mouth.

"Take him down to the livery corral and string him up over the gate."

They dragged him away.

People came streaming into the alley. One of them was a pouchy individual with a scraggly mustache and popeyes. He wore a nickel-plated badge on his vest and Bill knew him for Calder's marshal. He blustered, "Hey! What you fellers aimin' to do? If he's the one that shot John Turner I'll take charge of him. Turn him over to me."

They told him profanely where he could go and he followed them along the alley, arguing heatedly to deaf ears that he was the law and would take care of any prisoners.

Bill drew back the hammer of the Colt and tossed the gun aside; then he tore off a bit of cigarette paper and wet it and stuck it over the wound to stop the bleeding. His horse was standing a short distance away; Bill got on him and rode around the Frontier to the street. The whole town was seething. They had carried John Turner's body into the store and there was a crowd on the steps and the sidewalk in front of the building. Bill dismounted and tied his horse in front of the Frontier and went inside.

There was excitement here too, although it was subdued. The bartender who served him was nervous and jerky in his movements; the men along the bar were tight-lipped and for the most part silent. Their very silence was eloquent and their eyes glinted with something akin to satisfaction. Bill decided that they belonged to the "evil forces" that for some reason had wanted to see John Turner killed.

The doors swung inward and Calder's marshal entered. His face was red and his popeyes were more prominent than was usual. He stamped angrily past the bar, saying as he did so, "Monk inside?" The bartender nodded and the marshal rounded the end of the bar, rapped on a door, opened it and went in. As the door opened Bill caught a glimpse of a big, hard-faced man who was seated behind a desk. He had a mean face with a broad, squat nose, thick lips and heavy jowls. He had a glass in his hand and there was a whiskey bottle before him.

The marshal came out almost immediately. He closed the door and raised his voice, "Turner's men are takin' Sam Sneed to the livery corral to hang him. I aim to stop 'em. Any of you fellers that wants to come along put your right hands up and take the deputy's oath."

A dozen hands went up, the hands of everybody in the place, thought Bill, but himself and the two bartenders. The marshal mumbled some words and said in the same breath, "Come along." He pushed out to the street with them stringing after him.

Bill said to the bartender, "Mighty efficient marshal you got here in Calder. Raises a posse in no time."

The bartender poured himself a drink and downed it. "Yeah, Biff's a right good man."

"Biff?"

"Name's Bang. Cliff Bang. Fellers call him Biff."

"Biff Bang, huh? Catchy name for a lawman. Wonder why he didn't try to stop that shooting between Rafferty and Turner."

"Why should he? That was personal. Smoke and Turner had it, and Smoke told Turner to stay on the range where he belonged or come to town prepared to shoot his way out ag'in. Turner come."

"So that was the way of it. And this Biff Bang, does he always come running to Monk—whoever he is—when he wants to raise a posse?"

"Sure. Monk Malone's the mayor. Owns this saloon, too." He observed Bill intently. "Stranger in Calder, ain't you?"

"That's right. Heard of your nice little town and figured I'd like to look it over."

The man got a rag and started polishing the bar. "She's a nice town, all right. Stands on her own feet. Don't put up with no interference by Rangers and suchlike. Lots of fellers come here sorta for their health. If you got any troubles, pilgrim, just take 'em to Monk Malone. He'll see you through."

"I'll sure remember that."

"If you want, I can fix it so's you can see him."

"Don't bother right now. I'll probably get in touch with him later."

He finished his drink and turned away from the bar. He looked the crowd over casually, for more men had drifted in since Biff Bang and his army had departed. Most of the men he saw were hard-faced and well-armed and wore that air of unceasing vigilance which seems to go with those who walk in constant fear of attack or apprehension.

He went outside and walked to where he had tied his horse. A voice spoke at his elbow, "Excuse me; I've been looking all over for you."

Bill turned. The speaker was the pretty brunette he had noticed on the other side of the street.

CHAPTER TWO

BILL REGARDED HER for a moment in silence. He saw now that while her hair was as black as a raven's wing her eyes were deep blue. The top of her dusky head came just about to his chin, and she was even younger and neater and prettier than he had first thought her.

She said, "I saw you turn your horse and go back into the alley just after John Turner was shot. You must be the one who caught Sam Sneed as he dropped from the roof. What's your name, please?"

"Kriss Kringle," he told her solemnly. "But you may call me Kriss."

She frowned in annoyance. "You're a bit reticent, aren't you?"

He looked puzzled. "Does that mean I forgot my whiskers?"

"It means that you're reluctant to give your real name. But I'm getting used to that. We have so many faces in Calder without names. You are the one who caught Sam Sneed, aren't you?"

"It was nothing," he told her with affected modesty. "He emptied his rifle and two double-barreled shotguns at me, but I just took off my hat and brushed the bullets to one side, dived twenty feet and caught him by an ankle. I waved him around my head a few times and—"

"Just a minute! I'm afraid you fibbed to me. You told me you were Kriss Kringle and you aren't. You're Paul Bunyan. But before we get any further into this I guess I'd better explain."

"That might be a good idea."

"I'm not nearly so fresh and flip as you might think. My name is Molly Sexton and my father owns and publishes the *Calder Clarion*. I'm his star—and only—reporter. My curiosity is entirely professional, Mr. Kringle. Or is it Bunyan?"

He grinned. "Let's call me Bill Borden. Bill, to the press."

"Thanks, Bill. Now tell me all about it, won't you? You see, it's rather important. John Turner was the Cleanup Party's candidate for mayor and his murder has a political significance."

He considered her gravely. She was no longer smiling; there was pain and something akin to despair in her fine eyes. He said, "You liked him, didn't you? And you are heart and soul in this cleanup campaign."

"I did and I am. John was a fine man, honest and kindly. When I think of how he was first maneuvered into that duel with Smoke Rafferty and then deliberately shot down in the street I'd like to walk into the office of Monk Malone and empty a six gun into his fat body."

He nodded his sympathy. "Tell you what: I'll give you the story in exchange for the low-down on Calder. I'm interested. I've heard it called Murderers' Hole and The Devil's Doorstep and Hell's Back Yard, and I want to know just what—"

Molly didn't learn then what it was he wanted to know about Calder, for from some distance down the street came a sudden shouting and the sound of scattered gunfire. She turned and ran three or four steps in that direction, then stopped suddenly and shook her head despairingly.

"Darn it! I'm a lady and not supposed to run. At the same time I'm a news reporter and would like to know what's going on down there. What can it be, Bill?"

"You really want to know?" Bill ducked under the hitching rail, slipped the rein and stepped into the saddle. He reined the horse over to the edge of the walk and kicked his right foot free of the stirrup. "Hop on and we'll take a look at the battlefield."

She hesitated, flushing, and he grinned down at her a bit sardonically.

"Is the fearless reporter scared?"

She tossed her dark curls and returned his look defiantly. "For the sake of the press," she said, and gripped his outstretched hand.

He raised her off the ground and when her foot found the stirrup he slipped his right arm about her and held her securely. "Hang on," he said, and touched the horse with spur.

It is possible that he hoped to scare her; it is even possible that he expected her to cling desperately to him. She didn't scare and she didn't cling. Her eyes were bright and her dark hair whipped back in the breeze, but she rode relaxed within the circle of his arm, her chin held high and her lips firmly set.

It wasn't much of a ride. A hundred yards or so down the street and Bill swung the horse into a passageway which ran beside the livery stable. They swung around a corner and into the alley and found themselves on the scene of conflict.

Wes and his five cowboys were withdrawing slowly along the alley, presenting an unbroken front which bristled with guns. The marshal and his posse had taken to cover; Bill could see them crouching behind barrels and wagons and standing in doorways. When one showed part of his anatomy there was a blast of six guns calculated to convince him that discretion was the better part of valor. Over at the corral a man sat with his back to a post. He was nursing a broken arm and cursing monotonously.

A slug went *zing-g-g* over their heads and Molly involuntarily ducked.

Bill quickly reined around and headed back for the passageway. "We'd better be getting out of here or we'll be holding up a post ourselves," he told her. They put the stable between themselves and the battle. Molly Sexton had stiffened and when he glanced at her he saw that her face was chalk white.

He said, "I'm afraid our dauntless reporter is scared."

"And I'm afraid our dauntless reporter is slightly ill. Bill, did you see it?"

Bill had seen it. It was in the hope that she hadn't which had caused him to make so precipitately for the passageway. "It" was Sam Sneed, who so lately had hung by his hands from the roof of the Frontier and was now hanging by the neck from a rope attached to the crossbar over the corral gate. He was still kicking spasmodically and twisting about in the breeze.

"Sure, I saw it. Don't you think I'd better deliver you at the *Clarion* office so that you can write your story?"

"You can deliver me to the office, period. I won't be able to write until I stop quaking. And I think it would be well for you to put me down where I have something solid beneath me."

He stopped at once and lowered her to the ground, then dismounted and walked beside her, leading his horse. They turned the corner into the street, walked half a block, then halted before a one-story frame building with the words CALDER CLARION painted on the big front window. Bill tied his horse to a hitching post and followed Molly into the building.

There was but one room, but it was big and the front third was divided from the rest by a wooden railing. On Bill's side of the railing were two desks, several straight-backed chairs, a safe and a cupboard which served as a filing cabinet. Beyond the railing were a Washington hand press, a job press, a compositor's bench holding type, and the various bits of equipment and odds and ends necessary in the printing business.

Molly sat down at one of the desks and waved Bill into a chair. He drew it up and she found a pad of paper and pencil. "Now," she said, "the whole story and don't spare your modesty."

So he told her briefly of Sam Sneed's capture and she made notes while he talked.

"When you write it up," he said, "just forget the name Bill Borden. Make it Kriss Kringle or Paul Bunyan or Little Lord Fauntleroy, but don't mention Bill Borden."

She glanced up at him. "The mayor won't want to pin a medal on your chest, if that's what's bothering you."

"I wouldn't mind the medal; what I'm afraid of is that somebody might want to erect a monument to my memory, first making sure that I am a memory."

"Now who's scared!" she taunted. "The valiant hero who seized the villain by one leg and waved him about in the air!"

"Sure, I'm scared," he admitted much too readily. He grinned, then sobered. "No fooling, Molly; keep the Borden part out of it. I told you my name in a moment of weakness and now I'm asking you to forget it, *pronto*."

She said, "Oh!" and her face clouded. "I understand. Just another face without a name. Well, I'll keep your dark secret locked in my breast as a privileged communication." She turned suddenly stern and uncompromising. "Bill, if you're running from the law you'd better keep on running. You're safe enough now, but after election it's going to be different. Calder has sunk deep enough in the mud; we're going to drag it out and air it."

"We?" Bill's eyebrows went up.

"We. I don't care how bad a town is there's always folks who want to be able to look people in the face when they say where they're from. They're long-suffering and patient, but the time finally comes when they rise up in their wrath and drive the money-changers from the temple. There are dozens of examples: Abilene, Tombstone, Hangtown and others like them. In time they were cleaned up. And it was the decent element that cleaned them up just as the decent people of Calder are going to clean up this town."

"Hear, hear!" he applauded mildly.

Her cheeks were flushed with earnestness; now her chin tilted upwards defiantly and her fine eyes flashed. "Go ahead and laugh. Monk Malone and his gang are laughing too, but they'll find out!"

"From what I've seen Calder'll take a heap of cleaning. How are you going to go about it?"

"By peaceful means if possible, by force if necessary. The first Tuesday of next month is election day. We elect a mayor and three councilmen. Monk Malone has been mayor ever since there was a mayor; the councilmen change from time to time but only as Malone wishes. They play ball with him or something happens to them. The town marshal is appointed by the mayor and the councilmen and does just about as Malone directs."

"So I've noticed," said Bill. He sat with his feet out-thrust and his thumbs hooked in his cartridge belt, and he watched her from beneath the brim of his hat. She returned his gaze steadily.

"A man hiding from the law makes his arrangements with Monk Malone. That's pretty generally known, although it would be hard to prove. Malone takes care of him for a monetary consideration, the amount charged depending on the enormity of his offense against the law." She pressed her lips tightly together, then opened them suddenly and said, "Bill, what are you running from? What did you do?"

Bill looked startled. "Me?"

"Yes, you. Strangers don't ride into Calder to see the scenery. I want to know why you came here. What crime did you commit?"

He scowled at her. "Do I have to tell?"

"You don't have to but I wish you would. I promise that whatever you tell me will be treated as confidential. I'm hoping it won't be too awful."

Bill sagged lower in his chair and hung his head. "It was terrible," he said in a low, strained voice.

She leaned over and put a hand on his arm. "Tell me."

He looked up at her, misery in his eyes. "I set fire to an orphan asylum to hear the kids squeal."

"Bill!" She snatched her hand away. Her eyes were angry and her cheeks pink. "All right, don't tell me. Whatever it was I hope they catch you and give you a good long term in the penitentiary." She fiddled at her papers on the desk while he sat there grinning at her.

After a moment he said, "Sorry, Molly; but you sure asked for it. Gosh! I didn't know my villainy stood out on my face so plain. Why, I wouldn't be safe for a minute within sight of a lawman."

"It isn't that you look so much like a criminal," she said, "it's just that you came to Calder. Nobody but criminals come here."

"You and your father come to Calder."

"Dad's a crusader and loves to fight for the right. He moved here and started the *Clarion;* naturally I came along to help him. Reverend Ernest Rutherford came to preach the Gospel. He holds services in a tent at the end of town. His daughter Nancy plays the melodeon and leads the singing."

"And together you're going to reform Calder. Lady, you'll have a tough time persuading these roughs to vote the Clean-up ticket by tossing editorials and hymns at them. Only talk they savvy is gun talk and the way to persuade them is with a hunk of lead pipe."

"We're not wasting time trying to covert the roughs. We're doing our work among the decent people in the town; with their help we can defeat Malone at the polls. The cattlemen are with us; they're sick and tired of having their men come to town to be robbed, beaten and thrown into jail. They're tired of paying fines that go to enrich Monk Malone and his crooked justice of the peace. The cowboys will vote the way their bosses vote as a matter of loyalty."

"How about the tradespeople and the miners?"

"We're working on them. The tradespeople are scared of Monk Malone; he could have any or all of them boycotted by just passing the word. The miners are the real problem. If they'd turn out in force we'd win without any doubt, but the chances are they won't. They rarely stay in one location long enough to become interested in its politics; they hear of a new strike somewhere and off they go. Reverend Rutherford is working hard with them. He visits their camps and holds services. They adore Nancy and

I don't blame them; she's the nearest thing to an angel that you'll find this side of heaven."

"I've always wanted to meet an angel," said Bill dreamily.

She looked searchingly at him, but before she could speak the door to the street opened and two men entered. One was a rugged, carelessly dressed man in his forties; the other was not much older than Bill. He was well built, brown and handsome, with dark hair and moustache and flashing blue eyes. He was dressed conservatively but neatly.

The older man spoke quickly. "Molly, have you this awful story written up? We must get out an extra at once. John Turner died a martyr's death and the good element of the town is shocked and angry. I don't know what we'll do without him, but one thing is certain: his murder will swing many a doubtful vote our way. Malone had that man planted on the roof without any doubt. I wish we could come out and flatly accuse him of it, but as usual we have no proof. If Wes Peters and his men hadn't been in such a hurry to hang Sam Sneed, we might have got the truth from him."

"I have the material for the story and it won't take long to write it up. Dad, I want you to meet—this gentleman. He's the one who caught Sam and he's given us the story. Bill, this is my father, Leander Sexton."

Bill stood up and shook hands. Sexton said, "I'm glad to know you, Bill. That was quick work on your part; if you hadn't acted as promptly as you did we'd never have known who shot John." He turned to the other man. "This is Fred Sivart, Bill. He's one of the staunchest supporters of the reform movement."

Fred Sivart flashed Bill a quick smile and shook his hand. "We sure can use some reform in Calder," he said.

"Fred owns the Double Eagle saloon and gambling hall," explained Sexton. "Because of that he's a bit self-conscious, but I hold that a saloonkeeper can be just as decent a man and as good a citizen as a butcher or storekeeper. Going to be with us long, Bill?"

"I don't know. I'm just rambling around. I might stay a while."

"I hope you'll give us your support if you're here at election time. Meanwhile, look conditions over for yourself. They're deplorable. This town is rotten to the core."

"Your daughter's been explaining a bit."

"Molly's an ardent worker. So is Reverend Rutherford and Nancy. And that reminds me, Molly. We're holding a meeting at the Gospel tent tonight at eight. Rutherford is going to the miners with the word and I wish you'd circulate around town and notify the ones we can count on. We want to select a candidate to take poor John's place. I'll be busy getting out the extra but Fred has offered to get word to all the ranchers he can reach this afternoon and urge them to attend."

"I suppose you're keeping the purpose of the meeting a secret?"

"Yes. If Malone heard of it there's no telling what might happen." He glanced quickly at Bill. "Of course, I'm assuming that Bill is with us. I think he showed where he stood when he nabbed Sam Sneed."

"I'm as mum as an oyster," said Bill.

Fred Sivart said, "I'd better be on my way; I have a lot of territory to cover."

"And I must get out that extra," said Sexton.

"And you," said Bill to Molly, "must write your story." He turned to the two men. "Glad to have met you gentlemen."

Sexton nodded his acknowledgment and sat down at the other desk; Sivart gave Bill a nod and went out to the street. Bill leaned over Molly's desk and said solemnly, "Please, Miss Reporter, don't print anything about my burning that orphan asylum, will you? Lock it in your breast with the other privileged communications."

She frowned at him. "That was a dirty trick, Bill. Don't try it again or I won't be writing your story, I'll be writing your obituary."

In another moment she was laughing, and Bill went out whistling.

CHAPTER THREE

BILL GOT ON HIS HORSE and rode to the Frontier, where he tied and went inside. The members of Biff Bang's posse were lined up at the bar partaking of liquid consolation after their failure to save Sam Sneed. They didn't appear any too happy.

Bill walked along the bar and when he'd reached its end he asked the bartender, "Monk in?" just as had Biff, and the barman automatically answered "Yeah" before he noticed who had spoken. Then, suddenly recognizing Bill, he called, "Hey! Whadda you want with him?"

"That's my business, and his," answered Bill. He rapped on the door, then opened it and went in without an invitation from Malone. Malone was behind the desk and sitting in a chair across from him was the dandified gunman who was to have shot John Turner. They both stared at Bill and Monk said, "Who let you in?"

"The door was unlocked and I just walked in. You Monk Malone?"

"Yeah. What do you want?"

"Just dropped in to pay my respects. You busy?"

In addition to a big coarse face, Monk had a big, gross body. He didn't bother to keep the body tidy; his clothes were shabby and wrinkled and the string tie around the soiled shirt collar was askew, with one end dangling outside his waistcoat. He gave Bill a long, calculating look, then said to Rafferty, "That's all, Smoke. Tell him I'll take care of it."

Smoke Rafferty got up and went out through a doorway which opened on a passageway along the side of the saloon. He walked like a sissy, with small mincing steps. Monk scowled at Bill and said, "Well?"

Bill sat down in the chair Rafferty had vacated and pushed his hat back on his head. He said, "I'm a stranger. Just getting acquainted. Somebody told me you were the mayor of Calder and I believe in starting at the top and working down."

"What handle you usin'?"

"Bill."

"Bill what?"

"Anything. That's it, Bill Anything. Pretty, ain't it?"

Monk grunted and scowled at him. "You didn't come here to make jokes. What did you come here for?"

"Well, how about a job?"

"What kind of job?"

"Don't matter much, as long as there ain't much work to it."

Monk considered him, still scowling, and while he considered there came a knock on the door, then it opened and Biff Bang came in. He closed the door and stood glaring at Bill. He said to Malone, "This is the bird that caught Sam and turned him over to Wes Peters and his crowd."

Monk's eyes narrowed. "That right, pilgrim?"

"Sure. You don't need to thank me: I'm modest."

"Thank you! Why you damned fool!" Malone stopped abruptly, glared for a moment, then eased back in his chair and composed his features. "Just why did you horn in?" He asked it in a voice that was ominously quiet.

"I told you I'm a stranger in Calder. I'd just rode in and hadn't sized up the angles yet."

"And you figger you've got 'em sized up now, huh?"

"Partly."

Without taking his gaze off Bill, Malone said to the marshal, "All right, Biff; beat it."

Biff went out into the barroom and closed the door. Monk asked abruptly, "The law after you?"

"Well, you might say the law's sort of interested in my whereabouts."

"And you want a job, huh? That means you ain't got no *dinero* and want to work your way. Well, it might be arranged. What are you wanted for?"

"I kicked the stool from under a blind man and swiped his pennies."

Monk came to his feet, his eyes blazing. He leaned over the desk and shouted, "Don't get gay with me, *hombre!* I don't like it."

Bill glared back and answered just as harshly. "And I don't like people asking me personal questions. Not even the mayor of Calder. Think I spill business to every stranger I meet?"

For a short space their glances clashed, neither yielding; then Monk sucked in his breath and slowly resumed his seat. The anger in his eyes died; he gave a grunt that was half chuckle. He said, "You might do to take along at that. I dunno. I got nothin' for you right now, but stick around and come back in a week."

"Going to check up on me first, huh?" Bill sank back in his chair and fished out the makings. "All right; I'll stick around. But I got to find me some place to live. Got any ideas?"

"There's some empty shacks around town; pick out one that suits you and make yourself at home."

"Keno." Bill lighted his cigarette and stood up. "You handing me the key to your fair city?"

"I'm handin' you nothin' but some good advice: Step light and keep your nose clean. And next time somebody gets punctured don't be so damned curious. We got a marshal to run down killers—when we want 'em run down. Get goin', Mister Bill Anything."

Bill got going.

Now that he had met Monk Malone the situation in Calder was shaping up more clearly in his mind. The belief that Monk was protecting outlaws for a consideration was correct, although, as Molly had said, proving this to the satisfaction of a court would be difficult. The Cleanup Party had a job of work ahead of them. Molly Sexton and her father and Reverend Rutherford and his Nancy had the courage of their convictions, but they were up against brain and brawn and bullets, plus organization and a very understandable reluctance on the part of Monk Malone to surrender his authority and the income he enjoyed from the protection he gave fugitives from the law.

Fugitives from the law. Bill glanced about him as he made his way to the bar and saw those faces without names, as Molly Sexton had called them. Thieves, rustlers, swindlers, crooked gamblers, killers; all assembled in Calder for protection, ready to band together to keep out meddling lawmen if the need arose. Nothing short of a full company of Rangers would be able to ride into this man's town and clean it up properly.

Of course, should the Cleanup Party win at the polls there would be nothing to it. Give them the boost and the doubters, the timid and the inert well-wishers would all pitch in and help wholeheartedly. But let them fail just this once and they were licked forever, their prestige gone. They were staking everything on one throw and that wasn't good gambling.

Bill ordered a drink and while he was waiting for it a man slipped in beside him and he recognized Marshal Biff Bang. Biff asked, "How'd you make out with Monk?"

"I'm on a week's probation."

"That means I'll be watchin' you and checkin' on you. Don't give me the chance to get nasty. Sam Sneed was a friend of mine."

"You didn't have to tell me that. Maybe I'd better keep my eyes on the roofs for the next week."

The popeyes glared at him. "I don't haf to shoot from no roof."

"If I could depend on that it might save me from, a stiff neck. But you better consult Monk before taking pot shots at me. And it might be a good idea for you to make your will."

"You talk mighty big, pilgrim; but the loud-crowin' rooster ain't always the toughest."

Bill had more important things to do than argue with Marshal Biff Bang, so he didn't answer. He downed his drink and turned away, remembering that he had to find a place to eat and bed down in. He rode about the town, sizing up the various vacant shacks and fixing the geography of the town in his mind. He found a cabin that would serve and went to work on it. He bought a broom, a bucket and scrub brush, a supply of soap and a few yards of flannel. When he had finished the job the place was at least clean. There was a rusty stove and he cut some wood for it, then rode to the store for supplies. He bought food and candles and some grain for his horse. There was a shed behind the cabin that would do for his horse; he put the animal up, fed him, then cooked and ate supper and felt at home.

When he had washed up the dishes, he put on a clean shirt and scarf and rode to the Gospel tent, which he had located while searching for a cabin. It was early, but he heard the strains of the melodeon as he dismounted and tied a short distance from the entrance. He went into the tent.

A quiet gloom hung over the covered space with its rows of plank benches, its small platform where a table served as pulpit and the little melodeon a bit off to one side. Bill removed his hat, trod softly along the earthen aisle and sat down on the front bench.

Nancy Rutherford was playing something soft and sweet, improvising as she played. He could see her head and shoulders above the top of the organ, and some vagrant ray of light made a halo of her golden hair. She smiled at him and he smiled back and listened rapturously until the last chord swelled and then died. She got up and came over to him and sat on the bench beside him.

He said, "Why did you stop? It was beautiful."

"I saw you were alone and thought you might rather talk. You're the man who caught Sam Sneed, aren't you?"

"Yes." He was grave; one doesn't joke with an angel.

Her fair face clouded. "It was awful, so terribly awful. Both the shooting of Mr. Turner and the hanging of Sam Sneed. It wasn't really Sam who killed John Turner; the real murderer remains unpunished."

"Monk Malone?"

She shook her head at him. "It isn't for me to judge. I don't know. I only know that Sam himself had no cause to kill John. I'm sure he'd never even spoken to John."

"You believe that Monk Malone is behind all the evil in this town, don't you?"

"How can one be sure? There is no concrete evidence. All I really know is that the evil exists and it's the duty of every God-fearing man and woman to stamp it out. Are you planning to stay in Calder, Mister—?"

"Just call me Bill, Miss Rutherford. I don't think I'll stay very long, but I'll probably be here until after the election."

"I hope you'll vote for the Cleanup Party, Bill. Because of the shifting population there's no law regarding length of residence. Anybody who is in town at the time and wants to do so can vote."

"That's bad, isn't it? Monk Malone could import a bunch of roughs at the last moment and be sure of getting elected."

"Mr. Malone is entirely too confident of the outcome to do that. And it looks to me as though he'd already gathered in all the roughs available."

"Well, I sure hope you swing the election. I really do. And I'll help all I can. But you have a tough job ahead of you. Perhaps you're starting wrong; maybe it would be better if you get the law in here first to do the preliminary cleaning up. If you did that you'd win hands down."

"What law we have in Calder is entirely devoted to Malone," she said sadly. "The county sheriff is afraid to interfere. It would cost too many lives to do as you suggest. The Rangers might be able to handle it but they are few and scattered and too busy with more important matters. We've tried to interest them. Mr. Sexton wrote the most urgent letters and father wrote to the Governor himself. All they got in return was a vague promise of help when the necessary force could be spared. So, Bill, we must fight it out alone. At the polls. And we're going to win the election."

"I sure hope you do, Miss Rutherford." Bill really meant it.

"Please call me Nancy. Everybody does."

Reverend Rutherford came through a flap at the back of the tent bearing a lighted kerosene flare. He hung this on a hook on the tent pole nearest the pulpit, then came over to join them. Bill stood up and Rutherford extended his hand. He smiled and the smile transfigured his rugged face.

"This is Bill, isn't it? Molly Sexton was telling me about you. Are you going to attend the meeting tonight?"

"I'll be somewhere around."

"Good! We need the support of every honest man and woman in the community. You'll excuse Nancy, won't you? I want to go over the hymns with her."

Bill said of course he would and Nancy gave him a smile and a very small, soft hand. Bill took it gingerly; he had never shaken hands with an angel before. She said, "Come to see us any time, Bill. We live in the tent beyond, and you'll always be welcome."

Bill promised that he would and they went over to the organ. While they bent over a hymnal he quietly went out. It was getting dark now and he moved a short distance away and sat down on a sawbuck near the woodpile. He rolled a cigarette and smoked it thoughtfully. Nancy Rutherford certainly was one fine girl. Sweet and friendly and childlike, yet with lots of sense. She was the daughter of an evangelist, but if she converted souls it was by the persuasion of her own actions rather than by exhortation. She hadn't even mentioned religion to him.

People began to arrive for the meeting. They came singly or in pairs, unobtrusively and, he felt sure, unobserved by Malone's crowd, who would naturally be as far removed from the Gospel tent as they could get. Tradesmen with their wives and sons and daughters came on foot, as did the flannel-shirted miners; cowboys arrived on horseback but not in bunches as was their usual wont. Apparently everybody had been cautioned against arousing the suspicion of the Malone crowd. Molly Sexton, her father and Fred Sivart came together. Against the faint glow which came from within the tent Bill saw Rutherford standing at the entrance greeting each person as he arrived.

And finally it was completely dark and no more persons entered the tent, and Bill could hear the deep voice of Reverend Rutherford as he asked the Lord to bless those who had gathered in His humble temple and the cause for which they fought, which was His cause. There came the strains of the organ and the sound of voices raised in song. The hymn was a militant one, eminently fitting. It was *Onward, Christian Soldiers.*

Bill heard the mumble of voices but could not distinguish the words. He guessed that the regular prayer meeting had been deferred in order that they might discuss the crisis caused by John Turner's death.

The attack came without warning. A band of horsemen swept suddenly from the void behind Bill circling the woodpile and rushing toward the tent. One moment there had been comparative silence, and the next a very bedlam of sound. Hoofs pounded the earth, shrill yells ripped the air, six-guns thundered their contents through the canvas top of the tent. A couple of the raiders turned loose the horses at the hitching rail and sent them galloping in every direction. The marauders circled like Indians attacking a wagon train; the canvas shook and heaved, and above the shouts and gunfire sounded the cries of the frightened women inside. And then half of the tent collapsed. Somebody had roped the pole nearest the pulpit and had torn it from its moorings.

And the kerosene flare was attached to that pole!

Bill was on his feet, his .44 in his hand. He ran forward, firing at the figures that flashed by. He dropped one, saw a horse go down, then came a burst of flame as the canvas caught fire.

For an instant even the harsh cries of the raiders were stilled. The tent was blazing and there were people trapped inside. The knowledge appalled even the callous roughs who were responsible; they reined away from the scene of a possible tragedy and faded into the darkness.

From within the tent came cries of fear and confusion. The half of the tent nearest the entrance was still erect, and people began streaming out; but the half near the pulpit was down, coming to a peak some five feet from the ground where the canvas was held up by the table on the platform. It was just in front of this bulge that the flames were leaping into the air.

Bill walked up the yielding canvas like a man wading through a sea of molasses. He thrust his Colt into its holster and got out his clasp knife. He couldn't extinguish the fire, but he could stop it from spreading. He slashed away at the canvas, ripping it in a circle about the fire. By the time he had worked entirely around it his hands were scorched and his hair singed, but he had the satisfaction of seeing the blazing canvas fall to the earth and consume itself. The burning torch had fallen from the hook and was lying on its side, still burning. He snatched it up by the handle and hurled it out on the empty lot, then ducked under the canvas and worked his way toward the melodeon. He stumbled into the little organ, found a match and thumbed it into flame and looked about him. Nancy was not here; she had evidently got out in time. He crawled under the pegged-down side wall and into the clean air.

There was as much confusion without as there had been within. The women were gathered in a knot talking shrilly and angrily; the men rushed about in the dark as though expecting to find the raiders hiding near by; there was a small group gathered about the marauder whom Bill had shot, and another about the stricken horse. Cowboys milled about searching for the horses which had been turned loose. Bill started off in search of his own mount, and at the end of almost an hour found it in the alley near the Frontier. He guessed it had followed the marauders to their rendezvous. He mounted and rode up the street.

There was a light in the *Clarion* office so he dismounted and went in. Sexton, Rutherford, the two girls and Fred Sivart were there, and as he entered Molly turned and saw him. Her eyes were stormy and her face white with anger. She said furiously, "You certainly have gall to come here after what you've done!"

"And what," inquired Bill coldly, "am I supposed to have done?"

"You told Monk Malone about the meeting. You were probably with the bunch that came near to burning us alive!"

He said roughly, "You're as crazy as a coot."

"Am I? Who else could have told him? Who else knew?"

Fred Sivart said, "Take it easy, Molly. No good flying off the handle." He spoke to Bill. "What she means, Bill, is that you're the only outsider who knew about the meeting. You went straight from here to the Frontier and one of your informers said you were with Malone in his office."

A slow anger gripped Bill. But for him the tragedy might have been a far greater one. All that was needed to set them right was for him to tell his story and show them his blistered hands; but Bill was proud and stubborn and didn't give a hoot for the credit which was due him. Also it hurt to know that Molly would believe him guilty so easily.

"Sure I talked with Malone," he admitted harshly. "Who of you hasn't? I wanted to get the low-down on Calder. I don't know any of you any better than I know Malone. I heard your side of the story and I went to him for the other. Trouble with you is that you're a bunch of fanatics butting your heads against a stone wall. Well, go ahead and butt; the loss of brains won't be very heavy."

"You're so very right!" cried Molly furiously. "If we had any brains amongst us we'd have learned long ago not to take a stranger in Calder at his face value?"

Nancy crossed over to Bill, smiled at him and put a hand lightly on his sleeve. Then she turned to face them and spoke quietly. "We have no right to judge, Molly. None of us actually saw Bill with the raiders and news of the meeting could have leaked out in some other way. Fred mentioned one of our informers; Malone probably was his. Personally, I don't believe for a single instant that it was Bill who betrayed us."

She glanced about her a bit defiantly, then smiled up at Bill. The anger left him and he smiled down at her. He patted her gently on a shoulder.

"Thanks, Nancy. Don't you go butting your head against the wall. You, at least, have something inside it that you can't afford to lose."

He turned and went out into the dark street.

CHAPTER FOUR

BILL RODE down to Fred Sivart's Double Eagle and went inside. The Double Eagle was newer and more ornate in its furnishings than was the Frontier, and if the latter was the hangout for the outlaw element in Calder, Sivart's place was most certainly headquarters for the cowboys, miners and other adherents of the Cleanup Party.

Bill bought a drink and was sipping it when John Turner's foreman, the man called Wes, came up and stood beside him. Wes said, "I ain't thanked you for nabbin' that polecat for us. I'm doin' it now. The name is Wes Peters."

They shook hands. "Folks call me Bill. That shooting from the roof was sure bad business. Sam Sneed must have had it in for Turner."

Wes swore throatily. "Sam Sneed hardly knew John. He was planted there to finish the job in case Smoke Rafferty gummed it up."

"What started the trouble between Turner and Rafferty, anyhow?"

"It was a frame-up from the start. John was the Cleanup Party's candidate and Monk Malone figgered he'd play it safe. He done it through Smoke to make it look right. Smoke bought a hoss from John a couple weeks ago and later claimed the animal had been foundered and wasn't fit to ride. It wasn't so, of course, and even if it was Smoke had no kick comin' on a hoss trade, but he just wanted to pick a fight with John. One thing led to another and finally come to a showdown. Rafferty aimed to make a coward or a corpse of John, and John wasn't no coward. We fellers got wise to the setup and made up our minds John was goin' to get a square deal on the shoot out. We hadn't counted on somebody pluggin' him from the Frontier roof."

"What happens to John's ranch now?"

"He got a wife and four young kids. We'll run it for them, me and the boys, and if we ever get the goods on Malone we'll sure settle with him if we have to shoot our way through the Frontier to get at him."

"No proof that Malone was behind the thing, huh?"

"Not a lick. Everybody in town knows he's collectin' tribute for givin' thieves and killers protection, but nobody can prove it. That's the hell of it—knowin' it's so and not bein' able to prove it."

"Does Monk ever leave that office of his?"

"If he does it's at night. Nobody ever seen him on the street."

"I was wondering. Just before Turner was shot I saw somebody in the crowd on the far side of the street raise a white handkerchief and wave it."

Wes stared at him. "You mean somebody gave the signal for Sam to shoot? What did he look like?"

"I didn't see his face; just an arm and a hand with the white handkerchief. And I was so busy watching Reverend Rutherford that I didn't pay much attention. The fellow was in the crowd right behind Rutherford. You and your boys were on that side of the street and right close to him; can't you remember who was standing there?"

Wes thought for a moment, then shook his head. "No. We were all busy watchin' Smoke Rafferty in case he made a play. But Monk Malone wasn't anywhere near us, I swear to that. We'd of noticed him right off."

"Then if Malone planned it, he had somebody planted there to see that it went through. When is the funeral?"

"Tomorrow afternoon at the ranch. I come in to get John's body and arrange with Rutherford to conduct the services." He signaled the bartender for another pair of drinks, then said, "I hear some of the Malone bunch tore down the Gospel tent and set it afire."

Bill nodded. "The fire was put out before it did much damage. If you're looking for Rutherford, I left him in the *Clarion* office only a few minutes ago."

"Thanks, Bill. I'll be headin' thataway. Here's mud in your eye."

They drank and Wes went out. Bill wandered about the place, listening to the scraps of conversation, sizing up the inmates. At last he went out and got his horse and rode to the cabin. He put the animal in the shed, then went into the house, lighted a candle and closed and barred the door. He moved the table to a corner where he could not be observed through a window, sat down and put a wad of papers from his inside coat pocket on the table before him. He smoothed them out and began reading them slowly and carefully.

They were notices describing men who were wanted for various crimes, and some of the notices had the pictures of the men they described. Bill studied them, trying to match up faces and descriptions with the men he had seen in Calder. Four of them, he was sure, were even then in the Frontier, members of Biff Bang's posse, and a fifth contained an accurate description of Biff himself. There could be no doubt about it; the popeyes were a dead giveaway. The name was Cleve Bangor and he was wanted for armed robbery and murder.

There was nothing on Monk Malone, which was a disappointment. If Monk were wanted by the law Bill thought he might manage to get the man out of Calder and into the hands of the sheriff at the county seat. That would remove the core of the boil which was Calder. Of course, making Malone a prisoner, surrounded as he was by gunmen and knife artists, would be quite a man-sized job, and to attempt it without any definite charge to pin on him would be utterly foolish. At the moment it seemed that the only hope of convicting Monk lay in proving beyond any doubt that he was aiding and abetting criminals and sheltering them from the law.

A name on one of the notices had caught Bill's attention, and he read the circular several times. Name, AL TRAVIS; color of hair, blond; eyes, blue; height, five feet eleven inches; weight, 175 pounds. Six-inch knife scar on chest. There was no picture. The man was wanted for bank robbery and murder, twice over.

Why the name had arrested his attention Bill did not know. The description would fit any of a dozen men he had seen in Calder. The name held no familiar ring, but the impression remained that he knew the man if he could but place him. He ran over in his mind the men he had met since coming to Calder; the only ones whose names he knew were Sexton, Rutherford, Sivart, Peters, Malone, Biff Bang (Cleve Bangor), Sneed, Turner, Rafferty—He stopped there. That was all. Nothing that sounded like Al Travis, yet the name continued to haunt him.

He gave it up at last, pried up a floor board and put the notices under it. He undressed and got into the bunk he had fixed and lay for some time pondering his problem. He had met the leaders of the reform movement and the man behind what Rutherford called "the forces of evil;" he had gauged the determination and ability of the Rutherfords and the Sextons and had had demonstrated to him in the murder of John Turner and the raid on the Gospel tent the power of the machine they were bucking. It didn't look good.

Bill was no zealot and refused to contemplate conditions through rose-tinted glasses. He had been momentarily swayed by the enthusiasm and confidence radiated by Molly Sexton and Nancy Rutherford, and almost he had been persuaded that the Cleanup Party would sweep all before it; now, in sober contemplation, he didn't believe that was possible. Fair fighters never stood a chance against foul ones, and Malone and his bunch knew every trick in the book and were capable of inventing new ones if that became necessary.

No, the surest way to clean up Calder was by methods known to Bill and used by him in the past. *He must be rough and tough, and he would in all probability have to shoot to kill before it was over.* In the process he would probably earn the scorn and hatred of both these fine young women and the decent people who were associated with them; but what he did could not hurt their cause and what they did might help him. He must hold to his original plan if he would help make Calder a fit place for people to live in.

Having reached this decision, Bill went to sleep.

Except that the stores were closed, Sunday was like any other day in Calder. The saloons and gambling halls were wide open and did a thriving business, especially catering to the miners who rarely worked on Sunday. Bill moved about the town sizing up people, registering impressions, trying to match more faces to the descriptions on the circulars. He looked particularly for a man who might ring the bell as Al Travis. He did not find him. His tour took him past the *Clarion* office and he glanced through the big window to see Molly seated at her desk chewing on the end of a pencil. She glanced up, saw him, waved for him to stop and, jumping up quickly, hurried outside to meet him. She put out her hand and said, "Shake, Bill."

Wonderingly he did so. She twisted his hand and saw the blisters on its back. She looked up and there was contrition on her face. "I'm terribly sorry about last night, Bill. Really I am. It was you who put out the fire, wasn't it?"

"Nope. I got those burns playing with matches. My poor old mother used to warn me about it. I like to see 'em blaze up."

"Bill, you're the nicest liar I've ever known. Come inside a minute."

She drew him into the office and made him sit down by her desk.

"Nancy was sure it was you, and we all laughed at her. Then we found a man who had seen you throw the flare out on the lot. It made us feel pretty cheap. Bill, I want to make amends; I want to show you that we trust you, so I'm going to tell you a secret."

"Better not," he warned her. "I wouldn't want you to get mad at me again."

She smiled. "I don't think there's any danger of that. No I want to tell you. It's a closely guarded secret. At the meeting last night they voted to leave the selection of a candidate to Mr. Rutherford, my father, Fred Sivart, Nancy and me. We picked Tom Harrigan. He's a miner and a good citizen and his selection should go a long way toward persuading the miners to come to town and vote. What do you think of it?"

"You really want to know?"

"Of course."

"All right. I think that Tom Harrigan will be the next shooting victim."

"They wouldn't dare!"

"Why not? Killing off the opposing leader is always a good bet. And every death robs you of one vote."

"But they don't know we've picked Tom; they won't know until the last moment."

"That's the best time to pick him off. If you don't have enough time to pick another candidate the election'll go to Malone through default."

"Bill, you're the most discouraging person!"

"Maybe I am, but I know what you're up against. You're fighting thieves and killers who face arrest and conviction if they're chased out of Calder. In a way you can't blame them for not wanting to be chased. They know they're safe here because they've banded together and can make it so hot for the law that it isn't worth the cost in lives to come in after them."

He stood up and leaned over the desk. "Molly, you're too fine a girl to be mixed up in this rotten mess. You're going to see things that no decent woman should see. There'll be looting and shooting and mud and blood. Go away somewhere until the thing is settled."

She looked up at him, her color high. "I wouldn't think of it. Dad's in this with his whole heart and soul and I'm in it with him. Did you see the extra we got out?"

"No, I haven't."

She picked up a single sheet of paper printed on one side and handed it to him. He read it swiftly and handed it back without comment.

"Well, what do you think of Dad's editorial?"

"A nice piece of writing. Excellent tribute to John Turner and a swell condemnation of Sam Sneed, but nothing but vague hints that Monk Malone was behind the killing."

"We have no proof of that."

"You don't need proof that a tiger's dangerous; you know it. Look here, Molly. About this new candidate of yours, why doesn't your father run for the office? Not that I'd like to see him a target for Monk's henchmen, but he's a good man and would make a fine mayor."

"Dad's a newspaperman. He can put up a better fight for somebody else than he could for himself. And after Calder's cleaned up we'll probably be moving to some other town that needs us. I told you Dad is a crusader."

"Yeah, I know. Also I know that the crusaders failed in their mission. But I sure wish you luck."

"Aren't you with us?"

"Sure I am. But the time'll come when you'll probably think I'm not. You were mistaken in me once; I hope your faith is stronger the next time."

"Bill, what do you mean?"

He considered a moment, then said, "When you move into a house that's run down you begin your cleaning at the dirtiest spot. You don't wash the walls and woodwork and then start shoveling off the fallen plaster and broken glass and other filth.

I don't think you'll ever clean Calder through an election alone, and I certainly don't believe you're going at your job of cleaning in the right way. You're using a feather duster instead of a pick and shovel. Me, I'm a pick-and-shovel man."

The color in her cheeks was higher. She said, "Do you mean to stand there and tell me that you believe we should resort to mudslinging?"

"Sister, that's just what I'm telling you. If a fellow starts slinging mud at me, he's going to get it slung back at him; only I'll use more mud and sling it harder. And if he shies a rock at me, I'll shy a bigger and better rock right back at him. Now I'm getting out of here before I make you mad."

He gave her a grin and went out, leaving her sitting at the desk frowning after him.

So they had selected a miner named Tom Harrigan to run for mayor. Bill decided that he'd like to meet Harrigan and see for himself the kind of material they had picked. He got his horse and rode down to the gulch where most of the mining claims were located. A few miners were working, but most of them were idle. He inquired for and found Tom Harrigan's cabin. Tom was sitting outside the doorway smoking his pipe. Bill ground-anchored his horse and sat down on the bench beside him.

"Folks call me Bill," he introduced himself. "Harrigan, I understand you're going to run for mayor on the Cleanup ticket."

"Who told you?"

"Molly Sexton. In strict confidence, of course. I warned her that the other side might try to pull a John Turner on you. She couldn't see it. Have you thought about that angle?"

Harrigan removed his pipe and stared at Bill. The stare was not a friendly one. "I reckon I can take care of myself."

"In a fair fight I don't doubt it. The way the Malone outfit plays it you won't stand a chance. Turner thought that he did, and he was wrong."

"You're a stranger; what business of yours is it?"

"The election? None. I'll not be in Calder long and local politics don't interest me. But some mighty fine people are apt to get hurt, and that includes anybody who runs against Malone. I didn't think it would hurt to warn you to keep your eyes open and your gun handy."

"Does that warnin' come from Malone?"

"Malone doesn't give warnings."

"And I'm the kind of *hombre* that don't need 'em. I've stayed alive over fifty years by keepin' my eyes open and my gun handy."

Bill got up. "Sorry I bothered you. You live alone?"

"Yes."

"That's good. John Turner left a wife and four kids. Well, so long. Maybe you don't need the warning, but keep it in mind anyhow."

He rode away with the knowledge that while Tom Harrigan might be a good man he was also a stubborn one. He quite evidently resented advice from a man only half his age.

Bill did not attend John Turner's funeral. Many of the townspeople did, some of them trying to slip out of town without being observed lest they incur the wrath of Monk Malone. Bill was ambling around town when he saw Fred Sivart drive up to a little house near the *Clarion* office in a shiny new buggy. Molly came out and Fred helped her into the seat. She saw Bill and waved and Sivart nodded to him and got into the buggy beside her. They drove off and presently Molly's father appeared on horseback and set out in the same direction they had taken.

Bill returned to his cabin and went over the wanted notices again. He had identified two more fugitives from the law, but Al Travis still eluded him.

The uproar came rolling into the cabin like a tidal wave. It was in the form of yells and pistol shots and it came from somewhere near the center of the town. Bill hurriedly put away the notices and went out. He didn't waste time in saddling his horse, but ran to the main street. A mob was milling about the general store and he walked swiftly toward the place keeping on the far side of the street. The storekeeper, Henry Hollister, had gone to Turner's funeral.

The door to the building had been forced and the big front windowpanes smashed. Inside the store men were running about, tearing goods from shelves and counters and scattering them about. A rough was nailing a placard beside the broken door, but at the distance Bill could not read the words printed on it.

There wasn't anything he could do had he wished to, and the whole thing came to an end in a matter of minutes. Marshal Biff Bang came running along the street brandishing his gun and shouting at the raiders. They beat a precipitate retreat as though very much afraid of him, which in itself was rather ridiculous. Bill wondered if the whole thing wasn't a stunt to impress the citizens with the efficiency of Malone's marshal.

Biff came up panting and puffing; he surveyed the damage from the outside, then, gun in hand, went into the store and poked about. Apparently satisfied that there was nobody hidden there, he came out and seated himself on the steps like a faithful mastiff mounting guard over his master's property.

Bill grinned and crossed the street. Ignoring Biff, he halted at the foot of the store steps and inspected the placard. It was a square of white cardboard which had probably been purchased at the store itself, and on it was printed the legend MALONE FOR MAYOR. Beneath this, in smaller letters, were two short sentences: *Business is good. Keep it that way.* The printing had been done by hand and was a very good job, with the letters evenly spaced and shaped and the words correctly spelled. Not, thought Bill, the work of Monk Malone.

Biff Bang said, "Move along, pilgrim; the excitement's over."

"Ended," said Bill. "by the timely arrival of our valiant marshal. It was a nice show, Cleve."

The popeyes blinked. "The name is Cliff. Cliff Bang."

"The name is Cleve. Cleve Bangor."

The marshal's hand moved tentatively toward the Colt which he had returned to its holster, but stopped halfway there. Bill had made no move but his steady gaze was on Biff and the latter decided not to risk a showdown while he was seated. He waved a hand in a dismissing gesture. "Call me anything you want to, pilgrim, just so's you're happy."

"I'll call you Biff in public," promised Bill. "I wouldn't embarrass you for the world."

"Where'd you get hold of that name you spoke?"

"Read it somewhere. And it wasn't in a book."

The popeyes regarded him intently. "Just who are you, anyhow?"

"The name's Bill. Bill Anything. Didn't Monk tell you?"

The marshal did not answer and Bill moved to the wall of the building and stood with his back to it while he rolled a cigarette. Biff Bang, or Cleve Bangor, was on his left; Bill could draw and shoot across his body if necessary, but the marshal was in the awkward position where a quick draw was just about impossible. Biff watched Bill steadily as the latter twisted the end of the cigarette and lighted it. There was speculation and doubt in the marshal's eyes.

Bill side-stepped to his right until he came to the corner of the building, then said, "So long, Cleve," and slipped into the passageway and back to the alley.

Just why he had come out into the open with Bangor he didn't know; he had acted on impulse but didn't regret it in the least. He had given the enemy something to think about. He had made the first move in the game he intended to play.

CHAPTER FIVE

THERE WAS a great deal of righteous wrath on the part of Hank Hollister over the damage to his property, but there was little he could do about it except thank Biff Bang for preventing any further destruction. He did this grudgingly, knowing that had the roughs intended to make a real job of it the presence of Biff would have mattered not at all.

Nobody could be found to identify the raiders, which is not so strange when it is considered that the only ones who would have been willing to identify them were absent from town and attending the funeral. Biff blandly explained that the damage had been done by a bunch of drunks bent on having what they called a good time. Boys will be boys, you know.

Hank didn't protest too much; he repaired the door and put in new glass and called himself lucky for getting off so cheaply. He had read the placard and recognized it for the warning it was. Business was good and he wanted to keep it that way. To keep it that way, he gathered, he was supposed to vote for Monk Malone.

Nothing upsetting happened during the next few days. The Sextons were busy getting out the week's paper, which is issued on Thursdays. The Rutherfords held their regular revival meetings in a tent which had been patched and erected again, but the attendance would have discouraged anybody but the parson and his lovely daughter.

On Tuesday night they held a special meeting for the miners, transporting the melodeon to the gulch, where the earth furnished seats and the star-studded sky a canopy. Bill rode down there and sat his horse in the background, watching and listening. He told himself that his presence at the meeting was a necessary part of his plan to study the town and its citizens, but he knew in his heart that it was Nancy who drew him. He experienced a reverent regard for her which was entirely strange to his rather rough, unpolished nature. He wanted to be near her just to look at her and listen to her golden voice. It bothered him and sometimes it vexed him, but he couldn't help it. He told himself that he was getting soft.

Undoubtedly that meeting in the gulch gave the campaign of the Cleanup Party a big boost, for when the services were over Nancy sat for two hours playing and singing for the men. There were songs of home and mother and waiting sweethearts which brought tears to the eyes of many a hardbitten miner, and there were songs like *Suzanna* in which they joined, stamping their feet to keep time.

Bill continued to loaf about town, apparently taking life easy, but he did not relax his vigilance one bit. He knew that in recognizing Cleve Bangor he had started something and was fully prepared to meet whatever came up. If Bangor reported to Monk Malone that Bill had recognized him, the powers that be might decide that Bill was an undercover lawman, in which case there would be a speedy and probably a disastrous showdown. As the days passed uneventfully Bill decided that Biff had kept his own counsel and would act on his own responsibility if he considered any action necessary.

On Thursday the paper came out and Bill bought a copy at the store and took it home to read. There was the account of the raid on the store and the expected editorial on vandalism. Malone's name was not mentioned, which of course robbed the article of the punch it might otherwise have carried.

Bill met Molly on the street the next day and walked to the *Clarion* office with her. "I see you're still wielding that feather duster," he told her.

"What do you mean?"

"The lovely editorial on vandalism. You had the chance to lay out Malone good and proper and you muffed it. That vote-for-Malone placard hooked him directly to the raid, but instead of placing the blame at his door where it belonged, you went into a tirade against conditions in general, which everybody already knows are terrible."

"Bill, we just can't accuse Malone directly when we don't have a shred of proof."

"Afraid he'll sue you for libel?"

"He could."

"He won't. Try it some time and see for yourself. He'd have to bring suit in the county courts and that's the kind of machinery that Monk aims to leave strictly alone."

"You're the pick-and-shovel man," she told him tartly. "You told me so yourself. But I haven't seen any huge piles of debris being carted away."

"Give me time, gal. When I finally get going the dirt'll fly."

"Put off starting for two more weeks and we'll do the job for you. At the polls. I guess you read about the meeting in the gulch?"

"I was there, sister. I sat back and heard an angel sing."

"Then you know that we'll have every miner down there voting for Tom Harrigan. And that reminds me, Mister Smarty; the name of our candidate is still a deep secret."

"Want to bet?"

"Certainly! Only seven of us know it: Dad and myself, Reverend Rutherford and Nancy, Fred Sivart and you, and Tom himself."

"I hope you're right but I wouldn't make bank on it. I'll lay a good-sized bet with you right now that Malone knows. And I'll lay one twice as big that you'll never clean up Calder at the polls. They're too smart for you, too ruthless, too dirty."

"I'll take that bet and Dad'll back me. If by some strange chance we should lose, we'll sell the *Clarion* to pay off."

He grinned. "In that case you'll have to sell it to Malone. He owns just about everything in this town but a newspaper."

Saturday came and with it the termination of the week Bill was to wait before seeing Malone again. He went downtown shortly before noon and got a surprise. Across the front of the Frontier was stretched a strip of canvas on which was painted in crude letters FREE DRINKS FOR MINERS. It was Malone's answer to Rutherford's special service in the gulch.

Bill went into the place and bought a drink. There were not many customers, for it was still early. Smoke Rafferty and Biff were standing at the end of the bar and the marshal saw Bill come in. He went into Malone's office and came out almost at once and beckoned to Bill. Bill finished his drink and followed the marshal into the office.

Monk was behind his desk. Biff stood with his back to the closed door and Malone motioned Bill into a chair. Bill wasn't taking any chances; he moved the chair back against the wall and sat down, and when Monk raised his eyebrows in polite question Bill said, "I have right good ears; I can hear you over here."

Malone said, "You still want that job?"

"I sure do."

"Well, I got a little one to start you on. If you handle it right I might find somethin' permanent for you. You see the sign? Well, we'll have a flock of miners in here tonight and they'll get drunk and raise hell. Biff needs somebody to help him keep order. You're him."

Bill rubbed his chin thoughtfully. "So I'm the law, huh?"

"You're a hunk of it. Biff'll tell you what he wants you to do. Anything he says goes. Do as he tells you and you're settin' pretty. That's all."

Bill got up and turned to Biff. The marshal wore what was supposed to be a pleasant smile but Bill was not fooled because that smile did not reach the popeyes. Biff produced a deputy's badge and handed it to Bill.

"Pin that on you somewhere and report to me after supper."

That was all there was to it, but Bill was aware of a thrill of anticipation. There was something in the wind for that night and he was in on it. He couldn't even guess what it was; he'd have to play them close to his chest and use his judgment. It was the kind of game he liked. He pinned the badge on the inside of his coat and followed Biff from the room.

He went home, had dinner and came back downtown in the middle of the afternoon. Calder was filling up and miners were flocking to the Frontier, drawn by the free-drink sign. He went into the Double Eagle. There were some cowboys here, but the only miner he saw was Tom Harrigan, and Tom kept glancing across the street at the Frontier, temptation evidently tugging at him.

Fred Sivart was standing at the end of the bar and Bill said to him, "You'll have to put up a bigger sign offering bigger free drinks."

Sivart smiled wrly. "Looks like it, doesn't it? Especially if I want to go broke quick. Those miners drink like so many fish. How about having one with me? I could stand it."

They had a drink on the house and then Bill bought one. Tom Harrigan was still staring across the street. Sivart said, "Tom's body's here but I'm afraid his heart's in the Frontier."

"It's his body that we're worried about. You'd better see to it that he keeps it here."

He said so long to Sivart and went out into the street. He strolled along the sidewalk and when he was passing the store Molly Sexton came out. He tipped his hat to her and stopped for a moment's chat. This girl also attracted him. He liked the flash in her eyes, the quick movement of her head as she raised her chin, and most of all he loved to tease her and watch the play of emotions on her face.

"Pick and shovel still idle," she reproved. "Bill, I fear me you're a lazy workman."

"Not lazy; just a slow starter. Like an avalanche. I'm limbering up and getting ready to bust loose. Want an item for next week's paper?" He turned back his coat and showed her the badge.

"Bill! Where did you get that?"

"From Biff Bang, our noble marshal. Am I proud!" He started polishing the metal with his sleeve.

There was hurt in her dark-blue eyes. "Bill, you haven't! You just haven't gone over to the—the other side!"

"Whadda you mean, other side? I'd like you to know, young lady, that I'm on the side of law and order. This badge proves it. And don't let your woman's intuition run away with you, either. You did once, you know. Maybe I'd better take my nice new badge up to Nancy and show it to her."

"But, Bill, what does it mean?"

"I don't know—yet. I'm just a simple-minded deputy. I'll find out tonight and give you a full report. See you later."

He moved away before she could ask any more questions, and she gazed after him with a puzzled look on her face until the crowd had swallowed him. She shook her head and went her way. She just couldn't figure out this tall, attractive and entirely provoking man.

Bill ate supper at a restaurant to save himself the trouble of preparing a meal and when he had finished he walked back to the Double Eagle. Wes Peters and the boys from the Turner ranch had come in and were lined up along the bar. Bill wanted to speak to Wes but decided to play it safe. Somewhere in the ranks of the Cleanup Party was a traitor and he didn't want to be seen talking with Peters.

He stepped to the bar beside Wes, caught his eyes in the back-bar mirror and flashed him a warning glance. Wes caught it and did not turn his head. Bill ordered a glass of beer he didn't want and drank it without speaking. He got out a handkerchief and dabbed at his mouth and under cover of it said softly and quickly, "Meet me up at the store in five minutes."

He turned away and went outside and strolled up to the store. He went inside and bought some tobacco and was making a cigarette when Wes came in. There were several customers, and Wes halted at the counter two feet from where Bill stood. Bill said in a low tone, "You're honing to get back at Monk Malone and I'm going after him myself. I got to go about it in a way that most folks won't understand. Keep it under your hat; don't mention it to anybody. I'm telling you because when I need help I'll need it fast and bad. I'm counting on you and your men to furnish it."

Wes gave no sign that he had heard, but his answer came in the same guarded tone. "We'll be around. Day or night."

Bill returned to the Double Eagle and sat down in a chair near the wall. Tom Harrigan was still at the bar, having partaken of a liquid supper. The urge to join his companions in the Frontier was growing irresistible. Fred Sivart was watching him, but Fred was taking his trick behind the bar and couldn't be on the job all the time. Tom ducked out when Fred's back was turned, and he ducked out in a hurry. Bill got up and went after him, but Tom was halfway across the street by the time he reached the sidewalk. He called after the miner but Tom paid no attention, pushing through the swing doors of the Frontier and going inside. Bill followed him.

The Frontier was all noise and movement. Men lined the bar three deep and the games were running full out. Girls circulated among the crowd, soliciting drinks and gambling stakes. Harrigan elbowed his way to the bar and Bill walked over to join Biff Bang, who was seated in a tilted chair at the far end of the gaming tables. Bill sat down beside him and said, "Deputy reporting for duty, sir."

Biff was gazing intently toward the bar. He said from the corner of his mouth, "Get this and get it right. We're after one of them miners. We're goin' to put him out of circulation, permanent. Not now; the crowd's too thick. Pretty soon the fiddle and piano will strike up a dance. Them miners are suckers for dancin'. One of 'em ain't gonna dance. That's your part of the play, to keep him at the bar. Git into an argument with him, then tell him he's under arrest and flash your badge. He's drunk and he'll want to fight. Egg him on to drawin'. I'll do the rest."

Bill felt his back hair begin to prickle. He said, "What do you mean you'll do the rest? If the danged fool goes for his gun, what do I do?"

"Nothin'. Let him draw. I'll be at the end of the bar and I'll feed it to him. Resistin' arrest. By not drawin', you're in the clear. Makes it look better, especially with all these miners here. They ain't got no kick comin' if Tom draws first. Get it?"

Bill got it, but not exactly the way Biff intended him to. He saw at once that if Biff had any fear of him, of his knowledge of Biff's identity, this would be a grand way of getting rid of him without danger to Biff. All the marshal had to do was hold his fire and let the miner blast away at Bill. Bill, depending on the marshal, would be shot down before he could draw his gun. A neat little plan.

Bill said, "I got it. I let him draw and you plug him before he gets me. That means I must keep on the other side of him so we have him between us. Who is he?"

"Tell you in a minute; he's hid in the crowd now."

On the stage a fiddler began to tune up. Some of the miners turned to look expectantly that way. There was a short pause, then piano and fiddle struck up a lively tune and the bunch at the bar began to disintegrate. Miners gulped their drinks, seized the girls nearest them and dragged them to the small dance floor. When the supply of girls was exhausted, they paired up with each other. The three ranks before the bar became two, became one, became five or six scattered individuals.

Biff got up. His popeyes were staring and his jaws were tightly clamped. He made a motion to Bill and Bill got up also. Biff said, "There he is—the feller in the middle just takin' a drink."

The man was Tom Harrigan.

So Malone did know about the miner's candidacy. And Bill's prediction that Harrigan would be the next shooting victim was about to be fulfilled.

Bill knew he had to prevent the killing, but how? He could think of no way at the moment, didn't even want to. His mind functioned best in the heat of action. He said, "Keno!" and started across the floor.

He stepped to the bar on the other side of Tom, and Tom glanced at him and said, "You, huh?" He was the type that turns surly and suspicious when drinking.

Bill played his part. "Who'd you think it was—Santa Claus?"

"Mister Smarty Pants," sneered Harrigan. "The li'l boy that passes out the warnin's."

"You're drunk."

"Whosh drunk?" blazed Harrigan. "I can drink three smarty pants like you under the table." He raised his glass and Bill jostled his elbow, causing him to spill some of the liquor.

"What did I tell you? Drunk as a hoot owl."

He glanced past Harrigan. Biff was standing at the end of the bar; his feet were spread and braced and his right arm was crooked. Looked like he really meant to shoot Harrigan. But then he would have to look that way in order that Bill would go on with his part of the play.

Harrigan swore thickly and threw the rest of the liquor in Bill's face. By turning his head in time, Bill got it on the cheek instead of in the eyes. Harrigan followed up with a haymaker which, had it landed, would have knocked Bill into the next county; but it didn't land. Bill leaped backward and to his right, and Harrigan carried by his momentum, lurched away from the bar.

Bill snapped, "Hold it, you! You're under arrest." He threw back his coat, flashing his badge. He was looking at Harrigan but he could see Biff beyond the miner. Biff's fingers were on his gun butt and he was ready to pull. But Biff's gaze was not on Harrigan; the popeyes were watching Bill. That was the tip-off, and in that instant Bill knew what he had to do.

Harrigan yelled, "Arrest hell!" and clawed at his gun. Bill's hand dropped to the butt of his own .44. He seemed to be watching Harrigan but in reality he was watching Biff. He saw Biff's gun leap into his hand and swing around, but the half-inch hole in its muzzle didn't stop when it was pointing at Harrigan, it continued arcing around until it was pointed directly at Bill.

Bill leaped sideways three feet, and in the next instant several things happened. Harrigan, reactions slowed by drink, got his gun momentarily hung in the holster, Biff fired and the slug tore at Bill's left sleeve, and Bill tilted his swivel holster upward and fired through the open bottom.

He fired just one shot, then leaped forward and let Harrigan have a right that thudded solidly against Tom's chin. Harrigan staggered back a step, tangled his feet and sat down with a thump. He sat there staring, partly sobered, marveling now that he was still alive.

Beyond Harrigan, Biff was staggering toward the bar. He had dropped his gun and his knees sagged beneath him. He gripped the edge of the bar with both hands, trying to hold himself erect. He didn't have the strength. His body went suddenly limp and he collapsed at the foot of the bar.

The music had stopped and the dancers were staring. The men who had been at the bar were no longer there; some of them were behind it and others were under the gaming layouts. Bill walked over to where Harrigan sat, grasped him by the coat lapels and hauled him to his feet. "Sober now?" he asked.

Harrigan nodded, dumbly.

"Then get the hell out of here and stay out. And maybe the next time you'll listen to little Smarty Pants."

Harrigan started for the door, walking like a man in his sleep, and Bill crossed to where Biff lay and bent over him. The marshal was quite dead. Bill straightened and said to the bartender, "Monk inside?"

The man nodded, jaw sagging.

Bill knocked once on the door and then went into the office.

CHAPTER SIX

MALONE WAS SEATED behind his desk. Standing by a chair near the wall, poised and ready for action, was Smoke Rafferty. Smoke, Bill decided, was Monk's personal bodyguard. Bill closed the door and put his back against it and Monk said, "What's up? Where's Biff?"

Bill jerked his head toward Rafferty. "Order your watchdog back into his kennel and I'll tell you about it. He makes me nervous."

Monk said, "Set down, Smoke. This jigger's workin' on a job with Biff." Rafferty sat down and Monk said to Bill, "I asked you where Biff is. And what was that shootin' out there?"

Bill ignored both questions. He said, "Malone, what's the idea of trying to frame me?"

Monk's eyes reflected his surprise. "What you talkin' about?"

"You heard me." Bill walked over to the desk and leaned his weight upon it, looking down at Malone but also watching Rafferty. "You know the setup. Biff and I were to get Tom Harrigan between us; I was to make him draw and Biff was to plug him. Right?"

"I don't know how Biff had it figgered. If that's what he told you to do it was up to you to do it."

"That was the setup, all right; but when Harrigan made his play Biff shot at me instead of Tom. I jumped just in time and had to plug him before he could try it again. I don't reckon Biff'd do a thing like that without orders, and that's why I'm asking you why you tried to frame me."

Malone appeared to be genuinely astonished. "You givin' this to me straight?"

Bill indicated the tear in his coat sleeve. "I didn't do that on a nail."

"Sure it wasn't Harrigan's slug that done that?"

"Harrigan never got his gun clear. I knocked him down before he could draw. Ask anybody; they'll tell you about it."

Monk stared at him, then at Rafferty. Wrath boiled up within him and spilled over in words. "Why, that doublecrossin' polecat! What in the name of blazes made him pull a stunt like that?"

"That," said Bill grimly, "is what I'm asking you."

"Damn it! I had nothin' to do with it! The idea was to get Harrigan. They've named him to run ag'in me at the election. Now Biff's gummed the works and it's got to be done over and in a different way. Serves him good and right for gettin' killed. Or ain't he dead yet?"

"He's dead." Bill straightened slowly and took a deep breath. The plan to kill him instead of Harrigan was evidently Biff's and Biff's alone. He said, "Sounds all right, Monk. Maybe you didn't order it that way, but I wondered. I wondered because you picked me for the job instead of somebody like Smoke."

"We're savin' Smoke for bigger things," explained Monk. "When me and Biff talked it over we tried to think of somebody for the job and he said why not give it to you. I knew you were lookin' for a job and thought it would be a good way to try you out."

"Well, I've been tried. Like lard. What now?"

Malone hesitated. He seemed to be uncertain. He glanced at Rafferty, wet his lips, then looked back at Bill. "I—I dunno. I gotta think the thing over. You jest stick around; we'll find somethin' for you. Somethin' good. Jest stick around."

"Keno. But don't make me stick too long. I just shot your town marshal and if you don't want more of your crew laid up you'd better tell them the why and where-for and see that I'm in the clear. I'll be around when you want me."

He backed to the door and went out quickly. His opinion of Monk as a leader was a bit shaken. A good leader makes his decisions quickly; he doesn't stumble and stammer and postpone.

The noise in the Frontier was subdued. The shooting of a man was nothing new to Calder, but in this case folks were puzzled. Biff was a Malone man, which should have meant that his deputy was also a Malone man; yet the deputy had shot the marshal. To members of both factions it was plain that the whole thing had been a frameup against Harrigan, but the outcome had been rather startling. Both roughs and miners were uncertain. If the deputy had missed Harrigan and had shot Biff, that could be called an accident and Malone's followers had no cause for action against Bill. If the deputy had deliberately shot Biff to save Harrigan, the miners could have no quarrel with him. It could have been either way. The fact that Bill had evidently explained to Malone and had been permitted to leave Monk's office under his own power spoke for itself.

Biff lay where he had fallen. Bill glanced about the room and saw the bewilderment and uncertainty written on faces and knew that for the moment he had nothing to fear from either side. He started for the door, walking briskly.

A bartender called after him, "Hey, deputy! What'll we do with Biff?"

Bill answered over his shoulder, "Pickle him in alcohol and put him on the back bar." Keep it hard and tough; that was the way to deal with these birds.

He went out to find a small crowd collected about the entrance. Word of Biff's death had reached the Double Eagle and many of the patrons had come across the street to investigate. Among them were Fred Sivart and Wes Peters. Bill turned right and started up the street and the two men followed him. The street was lighted only where flares above doorways pushed back the shadows or faint illumination filtered through windows. At a dark spot Bill halted and waited for them to join him.

Sivart said, "What happened, Bill? I saw Tom Harrigan come stumbling out, is he all right? And is it true that you shot Biff?"

"Harrigan's all right. It was a frame-up against him, but Biff saw his chance to lay me low instead and I happened to shoot first. Biff won't frame another Cleanup candidate in this world."

Sivart was incredulous. "Why should Biff try to kill you? Was it because he thought you were working for the Cleanup Party?"

"He tried to kill me because I recognized him as Cleve Bangor, wanted for robbery and murder."

"How did you know that?"

"I saw a wanted notice somewhere and remembered him by his popeyes."

"Good for you!" said Wes. "That makes one less skunk runnin' around loose."

"And one less vote for Malone," added Sivart. "Bill, you're good; very good. The Cleanup Party needs more men like you. How are Malone's men taking it?"

"They haven't figured it out yet. Malone is sore at Biff because he neglected his chance to down Harrigan."

Sivart said, "I'm going into the Frontier and see how things shape up. Coming along, Wes?"

"No. I'll stick with Bill for a spell. Some of Biff's friends might feel sort of resentful and I wouldn't want to miss the excitement."

Sivart turned back and Bill and Wes continued along the street.

Wes said, "Bill, I'd like to get in on the ground floor with you. You got me guessin' a mite and I'd like to know more about the game you're playin'. How come you to be Biff's deputy to begin with?"

"Wes, I've told you all I can right now, and it's strictly between you and me. Also it's a lot more than I've told anybody else in this man's town. I aim to help the Cleanup Party, but I think they're going at it the wrong way. I'm used to fighting fire with fire. I asked Malone for a job and he gave me this one. I couldn't turn it down. Monk tells me that it was Biff who mentioned me for the job, which means that Biff had already figured out how he could get me without risk to himself. Now I have a toehold on the inside of the organization, which is where I want to be."

"You don't have to tell me any more than you want to, Bill. All I ask is that you give me and the boys a chance to help. John Turner was sure a white man."

"You'll have your chance. Do just as I ask without question and you'll be in at the finish. How far is it to the Turner ranch?"

"Not more'n an hour's ride if you're in a hurry."

"Could you arrange to be in town every night after supper?"

"I can and I will."

"Go to the Double Eagle, but leave it to me to get in touch with you. We don't want to appear to be too friendly. Malone has a spotter planted in the Double Eagle and gets his news direct. It may be the fellow who signaled to Sam Sneed with the handkerchief." He considered for a moment. "Is there a good strong outbuilding on your ranch?"

"The original stable was built of logs. It's still standin'. It's dark inside and the roof ain't much, but it's strong."

"Fix it up with doors that can be barred on the outside, will you?"

"I sure will." Wes was curious, but he did not ask questions.

They separated and Bill went on up the street to the end of town. He saw a light in the Gospel tent and heard the strains of the melodeon as Nancy practiced the hymns for the evening service. Bill went in. He liked to talk with Nancy; just the sound of her voice was soothing. He sat down on the front bench and when she saw him she stopped playing and joined him.

"I haven't seen you for days, Bill," she told him in her quiet voice. "I was hoping you'd drop in. What have you been doing?"

"Not much. Not until tonight. I went to that special meeting in the gulch. It was a grand idea. Win over the boys down there and you have a good chance of winning the election. And the one you've got to work on the hardest is Tom Harrigan. You've got to convince him that he has to keep under cover until after the election. Malone knows that he's your candidate and tonight he was framed and very nearly put out of the running. Tonight's plan went wrong; but the next time they may get him."

Nancy gave a little gasp. "You say he was very nearly put out of the running. How?"

Before he could tell her they heard somebody come into the tent and turned their heads to see who it was. It was too gloomy back there to distinguish the person's features, but Molly Sexton's voice called, "Nancy!" and then she came into the circle of light thrown by the flare and at the same moment saw them sitting together. She stopped abruptly and said, "Oh! Excuse me. A special meeting of some kind?"

Nancy said, "Come here, Molly. Bill just told me that Tom Harrigan got into trouble of some sort and I asked him to tell me about it."

Excitement shone in Molly's face and she was breathing quickly as though she had hurried. She sat down beside them, perching on the edge of the plank, tense and alert. "Well, from what I hear Bill's in a position to tell. Tell us about it, Bill. How did you happen to kill Marshal Bang?"

Nancy gave a startled exclamation. "Kill! Marshal Bang? *Bill?*"

"Yes, Bill. The whole town's talking about it. That's what I came to tell you. How did it happen, Bill?"

"Well," drawled Bill, "it wasn't much to brag about. Biff had two six guns, a shotgun and a knife. I just—"

She stopped him with an impatient gesture. "Yes, I know. You picked him up by the left leg and waved him around your head. But that was Sam Sneed; I want to hear about Biff Bang."

Nancy was looking at Bill and there was distress in her eyes. "You didn't really kill him, did you?"

He couldn't joke with her. "I had to, Nancy. Malone called me into his office this afternoon and asked me if I wanted to help Biff keep order tonight. I said I did and Biff appointed me a deputy. Harrigan came into the Frontier—they're handing out free drinks to miners—and he was pretty drunk. I saw he was headed for trouble and figured that if I arrested him I could get him out of there. But he got mad and went for his gun. Biff was behind him; he drew his gun and fired, but not at Harrigan. He shot at me. He missed, and I just had to shoot him to save myself."

"Bill, you're the most amazing man!" cried Molly. "I don't get it at all. Biff appoints you his deputy and then tries to shoot you for arresting Tom Harrigan. It doesn't make sense."

"Unless he shot at Tom and missed."

"At twenty feet? Think up a better one.

"Maybe he just didn't like the color of my hair."

Nancy was greatly distressed. She shook her blonde head sadly. "It's wicked, it's wrong. To kill anybody under any circumstances. Oh, why do men have to settle every dispute with bullets! Why can't they sit down and talk things over or thrash them out in the courts!"

"A fine chance Bill had to sit down and talk things over, with Biff throwing lead at him," said Molly.

"It's still wrong."

"Yes, I reckon it is," agreed Bill. "But most of us would rather be wrong and alive than right and dead. I didn't enjoy shooting Biff, but it may make you feel better about it if I tell you that Biff's real name was Cleve Bangor and that he was wanted by the law for armed robbery and murder."

"Now I get it!" cried Molly. "You recognized him as Cleve Bangor and he knew it, so he tried to shoot you. Glory be! When I tell Dad—!"

"You hold your horses," Bill told her sternly. "That's not for publication. Lock it in your breast with the other privileged communications."

"But, Bill, think of the story it'll make! Mayor Malone's pet marshal a murderer! Think what that would mean to the Cleanup Party!"

"Yeah, and think what it'll mean for me. More bullets. I can't dodge all of 'em. If you print that I'll take your Washington hand press apart and scatter the parts from here to Abilene."

"All right! Don't bite me. But surely it can't hurt to tell Harrigan's story. Tell me just what happened."

Telling Molly was entirely different from confiding in Nancy. Molly's zeal might lead her to print something which would lead Monk Malone to believe that Biff's deputy was entirely too free with his mouth. That would end Bill's tie-up with Malone and he was depending on that to worm himself into the organization. The information he needed could only come from within.

"Harrigan had no story," he said. "I told you he was drunk and didn't realize he was walking into danger when he entered the Frontier. The danger came when he got between Biff and me just as Biff was about to shoot. He might have stopped a bullet and ended any chance of being Calder's mayor."

"A little farfetched, isn't it? The Frontier was handing out free drinks to miners. Tom's a miner. I don't see how he'd be in any more danger than any other miner."

"He was in danger," said Nancy quietly, "because Malone knew that he was the Cleanup Party's candidate for mayor."

"But that's impossible! Only seven—"

"Sure," said Bill. "Only seven of us are supposed to know that. But you told me and maybe somebody else told a friend of his. Maybe Tom himself talked. At any rate, the word got around to Malone. That means I win one of those bets I made with you. What you've got to do now is convince Tom that he's in danger every minute, every second. I tried to warn him, but he gave me the brush-off. Said he could take care of himself." He got up. "I must be trotting along. So far as I know I'm Biff's only deputy, which means that I am now the law in Calder. Treat me with the proper respect."

Molly got up also. "I don't know how to treat you. One moment I think you're for us one hundred per cent, and the next I'm just as sure you're against us. Would your majesty deign to permit a humble reporter to walk as far as her office in your company?"

Bill said he reckoned his majesty could stand it, and they said good night to Nancy and left the tent together. They walked in silence for some distance, then Molly said, "That was a frame-up against Tom Harrigan tonight, and you were a party to it."

"My, my, the imagination these newspaper reporters have!"

"Don't try to laugh it off. It has all the earmarks of a frame-up. You were to arrest Harrigan knowing he was drunk and would start a fight; then Biff was to shoot him down for resisting arrest."

She was keen, all right. Bill said, "I told you Biff shot at me."

"I heard you. I'm even inclined to believe you, since you had discovered Biff's identity. But suppose he had actually shot at Tom?"

"I didn't aim to let him shoot Tom. Knowing Biff was a murderer, I'd have winged him before he could do it."

"And how would you have explained that to Malone?"

"I'd have said I thought Biff was aiming at me."

"You're a bit careless with the truth, aren't you? Even with me. I never know when you're telling the truth. I don't know at this minute where you stand. Certainly if you went into that frame-up with your eyes open you belong with the other thugs on Malone's side."

Bill sighed. "Sister, I always go into things with my eyes open. It's you who's blind. You jump at conclusions. I hate to remind you of it, but you do remember the Gospel tent, don't you?"

They had reached the *Clarion* office and had halted. She put her hand on his arm and when she spoke again her voice was repentent. "Yes, Bill, I remember. Forgive me. The way information leaks out is just getting me down."

"Your outfit isn't careful enough. In your enthusiasm you talk, and somebody is carrying every word you say to Malone."

"I suppose you're right. We'll just have to be more careful." She stood for a moment thinking, then said, "I told Father what you thought about our editorials. We're going to change with the next issue. We're going to come right out and lay the blame on Malone and accuse him openly of harboring criminals for a price."

"You can do better than that. I'll withdraw my request that you don't print Harrigan's story. Come right out and accuse Malone of framing him, with Marshal Bang and his deputy all set to get him. You can say that for some reason, probably personal, the marshal decided to shoot the deputy and got plugged himself."

"Isn't that putting it a bit too strong?"

"Not at all. It's no more than the crowd in the Frontier guesses. Mail copies of that editorial to the Governor, the County Attorney and the Sheriff. If Monk sues you, at least the whole miserable mess will be dragged into the open. But Monk won't sue; I'll make another little bet with you on that."

"No, you won't. You're too often right. But not about the election. I'd bet the *Clarion* on our winning that."

"Well, I haven't enough money to cover the bet, but I have plenty of time. I'll bet a lifetime of service against the *Clarion*. If the Cleanup Party wins the election you can order me around for the rest of my life. Now how does that strike you?"

"I'll take that bet. I've always wanted a butler."

They shook hands on it.

CHAPTER SEVEN

BILL WENT on down the street, the people he passed eying him curiously. They didn't know just where he stood, which was a situation not without its dangers. Straddling the fence is ever a perilous game, with the prospect of both sides striking at you ever present. His capture of Sam Sneed had precipitated him into the mess before he had had a chance to get his bearings, and now he was faced with the problem of protecting Molly and Nancy and their friends and at the same time apparently giving his all for Monk Malone.

He entered the Frontier and stood just within the doorway looking about him. The place was humming again, with the two-piece orchestra going full blast and miners lumbering about the dancing floor like so many determined grizzly bears. The air was thick with smoke and dust. Biff's body had been removed and new sawdust sprinkled over the spot where he had lain.

Bill crossed to the bar and ordered a drink. While he was pouring it from the bottle the door to Malone's office opened and Smoke Rafferty came out. He surveyed the crowd and when he saw Bill he crooked a finger at him and jerked his head toward the office. Bill finished his drink and followed Smoke inside. In addition to Malone there were three other persons present.

Monk said, "Howdy, Bill. Meet up with Ed Dillon, Frank Cade and Pete Stacy. Ed runs the Lucky Tiger, Frank banks faro in the Double Eagle and Pete owns the livery corral. The three of 'em make up the town council and I got 'em together at once because of Biff's checkin' out."

Bill nodded to the three and got nods in return. Ed Dillon was a big, surly man with a luxurious mustache, plastered-down hair and perpetual scowl; Frank Cade looked like the gambler he was; Pete Stacy had associated with horses for so long that he had come to look and smell like one. He had a long face and sad eyes and a forelock that dangled over the bridge of his nose.

"The council," said Monk, "have voted to put you in as town marshal. Salary is a hundred a month. Suit you?"

"It'll do. I work alone?"

"Mostly. If you need help you come to me. I'll find you a deputy." He indicated a badge and a bunch of keys which lay on his desk. "Jail's alongside of Ed's Lucky Tiger. Nobody in it right now. Across the street from it is Judge Higby's office. He's justice of the peace. When you run anybody in take 'em right over and he'll try 'em."

Monk filled a tumbler half full of whiskey from the bottle on his desk, downed it in a long gulp, then pushed bottle and glass toward Dillon. "Have a drink to the new marshal, boys."

They drank in turn. Bill took his direct from the bottle. He didn't know much about germs but doubted that even the rotgut liquor would kill the kind that Monk and Dillon and Stacy bred. Frank Cade, the gambler, was outwardly clean.

"Reckon that'll be all, boys," said Monk pointedly, and the three councilmen got up. They shoot hands with Bill and went out, and at a signal from Malone, Rafferty went out with them.

Monk said, "Set down, Bill. Got a little business to talk over."

When Bill had straddled a chair, Malone went on: "You come to Calder for protection and you come to the right place. Ain't nobody goin' to bother you here. But naturally that protection's gonna cost you somethin'. You'll kick back with half of that hundred bucks a month to me."

"Says who?"

"Says me. Feller like you can get along fine on fifty bucks a month and no worries. And they's plenty comin' in on the side.

You arrest 'em and get twenty-five per cent of the fines. Runs into money."

"Who gets the other seventy-five per cent?"

"Higby gets twenty-five and the organization gets fifty."

"Don't leave much for the town, does it?"

"Town don't need money. No sewers or street pavin' to lay or other fancy things. Merchants chip in to pay your salary and mine."

"What does the organization need money for?" Bill thought he knew, but he wanted to get it straight from Monk.

"You'll find out if a sheriff's posse ever rides into Calder after you. That *dinero* will hire enough guns to lick the United States Army and most of the Navy."

"I see. Okay, it's a deal." Bill got up, took the marshal's shield and pinned it where the deputy's badge had been, then put the latter and the keys into his pocket.

Monk said, "I hear you're right friendly with the Cleanup boys and gals. That's all right as a bluff; you might hear somethin' we'd like to know about. Looks better too, your bein' marshal. Shows we ain't playin' no politics where the good of the town's concerned." He grinned and gave Bill a merry wink.

Bill said, "I know them to speak to and that's about all."

"Yeah? Ain't the way I heard it. But that's your affair. Just so you don't go passin' information to 'em. I'll find out about it if you do and then you'll have somethin' to worry about. That Rutherford gal's some dish, ain't she? Too bad she's so danged religious. But mostly them kind sorta forget their bringin'-up when a good-lookin' feller comes along."

Bill had the impulse to plant a hard fist squarely on the thick, grinning lips, but that would be foolish, of course.

Monk went on. "Molly Sexton ain't too bad, if you like 'em dark; but Fred Sivart's got her corralled and ready for brandin'. Nice feller, Fred, even if he has throwed in with the Cleanup bunch. He went in with 'em on her account, of course, so you can't blame him too much. Well, good huntin'."

Bill said he hoped so and went out. He had had it straight from Monk's mouth that protection was being given criminals for a price; but he still lacked the proof that would hold up in court. He saw Smoke Rafferty standing near the end of the bar and moved in beside the gunman and ordered a drink. Rafferty turned back Bill's coat and glanced at the badge. "So you're the new town marshal. Feel right proud, don't you?"

"Not particularly. All that badge means to me is grief."

"And a hundred bucks a month."

"Less fifty for the cause."

"Plus protection. But get this, feller: that protection's only against outsiders. In Calder you stand on your own feet, and you'd better step light. Don't start treadin' on any toes. Biff had a lot of friends, and I'm one of them."

"Don't let your grief over his passing make you careless, Smoke."

Rafferty glared at him, but Bill had all the advantage at the moment. He was standing at Rafferty's right and Smoke would have to step back before he could draw. Bill could simply pivot and tilt up that swivel holster and let go. He picked up his drink with his left hand, downed it, passed behind Rafferty and walked toward the door. He knew that Smoke would not shoot him in the back; Smoke was proud of his reputation as a gun fighter and would scorn to take an advantage.

Bill went up the busy street, weaving through the crowd until he reached the *Clarion* office. Molly was seated at her desk working by the light of a lamp. He pushed open the door and thrust his head inside.

"Item for the paper," he said. "I been promoted. Hundred a month and cemetery reservation on Boot Hill." He threw back his coat. "Ain't it pretty?"

He got a kick out of the surprise which flashed in her eyes. She got up and came over to the doorway, the surprise changing to a frown as she saw the word MARSHAL on the badge.

"That does it," she said. "You've thrown in with them, haven't you?"

"You don't like it? Why, the town council elected me. Mr. Malone showed himself a square shooter. He knew I was mixed up with you folks and made me marshal to show that he never plays politics where the welfare of Calder's concerned."

She stared at him with fire in her eyes and her lips tightly compressed.

"Of all the things I ever heard, that's just about the limit! Monk Malone a square shooter! Bill, how did you get that badge?"

"I told you. Monk called a meeting of the council and they appointed me marshal. Seems that I got to work for my protection. You know—that orphan asylum. G'night!"

He closed the door and went up the street, leaving her more puzzled than ever. He was chuckling; he sure loved to stir her, to see the fire in her eyes, to hear her sharp retorts. He was flint and she was steel and the sparks never failed to fly.

He heard the commotion at the Gospel tent while he was still half a block away. There was a kerosene flare at the entrance to the tent and beneath it he could discern some half a dozen grouped figures. From their midst came a raucous cry like that of a barker at a side show, "Hur-ry, hur-ry, hur-ry! Put your money on the table and pick the shell with the little pea beneath it. I pay two to one if you can do it. It's easy—easy! Step right up, gents, and try your skill!"

Bill broke into a run and as he drew near he saw that a shell artist had set his layout up before the tent. The six men who had gathered before the table were Malone roughs. It was certain that Reverend Rutherford could not conduct services with this uproar so near. As Bill approached the entrance he saw the preacher come out to remonstrate with the barker. Rutherford put a hand on the man's shoulder and said something to him.

The man wheeled. He was a stocky fellow with a red face. He wore flashy clothing and a beaver hat. Bill heard him say, "Good evening, Parson. Step right around to the front of the table if you want to try your skill. Double your money in two shakes."

Rutherford's deep voice replied, "My friend, you mustn't do this. You are interfering with our worship. Take your game elsewhere."

"Not on your tintype! This is a free country, Parson, and this lot belongs to the town. I got as much right to use it as you have." He turned his back to Rutherford and once more launched into his spiel.

Rutherford's big hands clenched at his sides and Bill saw the flame which leaped into his eyes. He controlled himself with an effort and once more appealed to the man. "My friend, I tell you this must stop. At once. This is the house of the Lord; you must not defile it."

A big rough among the six on the far side of the table stepped forward, hitched his gun belt and said, "Aw, go roll your hoop, Parson. I got a buck here that says I can pick out the little pellet."

He slapped a silver dollar on the table and the dealer instantly put two dollars with it. He put a pea on the table, covered it with one of the shells, then rapidly manipulated the three shells for a few seconds and raised his hands. "Take your pick, sir. If you uncover the pea, the money is yours."

The rough raised one of the shells. The pea was not beneath it. The gambler pocketed the three dollars, saying, "The hand is quicker than the eye. Try again, friend. It's easy once you get the hang of it."

Rutherford let the tautness go out of his huge frame and his shoulders sagged. He was strong enough to break the gambler in two, but he was not a man of violence. Bill stepped around to the entrance and saw Nancy standing a little behind her father. Her eyes were fixed on the preacher and there was sympathy and pain in them; then she turned her head and saw Bill and her face brightened. She came swiftly to where he stood.

"Bill, is there anything you can do to stop this? It's deliberate, of course. They're trying to break up our services."

Bill gave her a tight, reassuring smile and stepped up to the gambler. The man's spiel stopped abruptly as Bill's hand fell on his shoulder. He wheeled swiftly and Bill flashed his badge. The man stared at it and Bill said, "The good old shell game, huh? And six suckers anxious to take the bait."

The big rough growled, "Who you callin' suckers?"

"I'm looking right at you, Bud. You ought to know you couldn't pick out that pea in a thousand years if this tinhorn doesn't want you to. I'll show you why, in case you're still wet behind the ears."

He brushed the gambler to one side and stepped up to the table. The man seized his arm in an effort to stop him, and Bill turned a cold pair of eyes on him. "Keep your fingers off me, tinhorn, or I'll slap your ears around to the back of your head." The man dropped his hand and Bill turned the other two shells over. There was no pea on the table.

"Yes," said Bill, "the hand is quicker than the eye, and in this case the foot is quicker than either of them. All the tinhorn has to do is run the shell with the pea under it over this spot." He indicated a little circle on the surface of the table. "Then he presses on a foot pedal, like this." He pressed on the pedal and a small plug was withdrawn leaving a small circular hole. "The pea drops through this hole, runs along a little chute to a cup. Very easy, isn't it?"

The roughs did not appear to resent the trick which was being played on them, which, of course, showed that the whole scheme had been worked out beforehand. The big one said, "We like it. You run along and help the Parson peddle his papers. Go on, pilgrim; get goin'."

His hand dropped to his gun in what would have been a remarkably swift draw had it been completed. He didn't even get the gun out of its sheath. Bill's swivel holster tipped up and the big man saw the muzzle of the .44 looking at him. He took his hand off his gun butt as though it had suddenly turned red-hot, and he drew his heavy brows together in a scowl. "Gun artist, huh?" he grated. "Well, you can't get away with it. Monk Malone made you marshal and he can unmake you just as quick."

"He won't," Bill assured him with more confidence than he felt. "One of my duties is to protect you poor, innocent little boys from crooked gamblers and confidence men. Reverend Rutherford, will you kindly collect the hardware?"

He said it over his shoulder, holding the six men under his hard gaze, the holster still tilted upward. Rutherford stared at him for a moment, then went around the table. Bill said, "Unbuckle your belts and pass them over to the preacher."

The big man said, "I'll be damned if I will!"

Bill thrust out his chin and looked savage. A double click sounded as he drew back the hammer of the Colt. "I said unbuckle your belt and pass it over to the preacher."

The big man slowly unbuckled the belt, his hands trembling with rage, and Rutherford took the belt from him and turned to look inquiringly at Bill.

"Get the others, too."

Each man in turn unbuckled his belt and handed it to the preacher.

When they had been disarmed Bill said, "What you boys need is a little religion. You're going inside and listen to a good sermon. Follow Reverend Rutherford into the tent. When the services are over you'll get your weapons back. Start moving."

Rutherford's face broke into a smile and his eyes lighted up. Bill could not see Nancy but he could almost feel her approval. The big man glared but Bill glared harder and said, "You're going in—vertical or horizontal. If it's horizontal, the rest of us'll listen to your funeral oration."

The big man turned and stepped into the tent after Rutherford. The others followed sheepishly. Bill said to the shell artist, "You need some converting, too. Step right along." Bill brought up the rear and Nancy fell in beside him and took his arm. Her eyes were bright and her lips curved in a warm smile. She whispered, "God will forgive you much for this, Bill."

There were two dozen or so people in the tent, mostly women, and they stared round-eyed at the procession. Bill said softly, "Right up to the front, boys, and don't crowd. And take off your hats."

All of them obeyed the latter order but the big man. They filed around the end of the front bench and seated themselves stiffly, uncomfortably. Nancy went to the organ and Rutherford mounted the dais and laid the belts on the floor beside the pulpit. Bill sat down in the second row immediately behind the big man; he reached out and took the fellow's hat from his head and got a glare of hatred for his reward.

Nancy played the opening bars of *Just As I Am* and the congregation sang. They sang standing, and the roughs also stood, although it took a prod in the back with Bill's gun to get the big man on his feet.

Nancy got up from the organ and came to the front of the congregation with a small wicker basket in her hand. She passed the first two benches without stopping, then started taking up the collection. When she had finished and had returned to the front, Bill got up and said softly, "Let me have it." She gave him the basket. He held it in his left hand; his right rested on the butt of the gun in the swivel holster. He said, "Shell out, boys. And be right liberal. The Lord loveth a cheerful giver." The first one was the shell artist; he fumbled about in his pocket but could find nothing but silver dollars. Reluctantly he tossed one of the coins into the basket.

The others, not to be outdone, were equally generous. All but the big man. He scowled at Bill and refused to give. Bill said, "I'll help pay your way into heaven," and put in two dollars. He handed the basket to Nancy and returned quietly to his seat.

Reverend Rutherford preached. He told them the story of the prodigal son. He told it in simple words, and in spite of themselves the men in front of Bill were interested. All but the big fellow. He sat straight and scowling and belligerent. When Rutherford said, "Let us pray," all but the big man kneeled at once. Bill nudged him persuasively with the .44 and the big man knelt also.

They sang again, and Bill was surprised when several of his reluctant worshipers joined in. When Rutherford asked the blessing of the Lord upon them, they stood with bowed heads. All but the big man. Rutherford pronounced the benediction and came down to them, smiling, and shook their hands. The big man shoved both hands into his pockets and glared.

"I'm glad you were with us," Rutherford told them earnestly. "I wish you'd come again. We're just peaceable folk who ask no more than to worship in peace and quiet. Get your weapons and go your ways with my blessing."

They wished him good night a bit sheepishly, got their guns and tiptoed from the tent. Bill stood at one side watching the big man. He snatched up his gunbelt, buckled it about him, then slouched over to Bill to get his hat. He slapped it on his head and said, "You ain't seen the last of me, feller. I was a friend of Biff's and I don't like the way you look or talk or walk or anything about you. Next time you see me, start shootin'."

"It'll be a pleasure," said Bill politely. "Good night and pleasant dreams."

The big man stamped along the aisle, thrusting aside the people who were in his path. Rutherford had gone to the entrance to wish the congregation good night. Nancy came up to where Bill stood and laid her hand on his arm. He looked down at her and sighed. "I get into the worst messes, don't I, Nancy?"

Her eyes were shining. "I think you're the most splendid man in the world, Bill. Some of those men were really repentant; I could see it in their faces."

"It won't last. They'll get over it with the first shot of liquor."

"Maybe. But if just one of them would really repent there would be rejoicing in heaven."

"There's one sinner in that bunch that there won't be any rejoicing over. And if he don't change his ways mighty sudden he's going to be standing before Saint Peter before he knows it. You heard what that big bruiser said to me?"

"To—to start shooting the next time you saw him? Yes, I heard, Bill. You'll be careful, won't you?"

"Of course. But I can outshoot him with one hand tied behind me, and he isn't fit to live anyhow."

"You mustn't say that. Bill, promise me you won't kill him."

He was astonished. "How can I? The next time we meet I'll have to shoot him or be shot myself. I can't promise anything as foolish as that, Nancy."

"You could avoid meeting him."

"And let him go around flapping his wings and crowing? Nancy, I don't understand you. You're a fine girl and I respect you for the real Christian that you are; but I thought you were intelligent. I just can't picture you as a fanatic."

She did not look at him, nor did she answer him directly. She was gazing toward the tent entrance and her voice was very low when she spoke. "There was a boy once. He was a young, happy-go-lucky, with curly brown hair and laughing eyes. You remind me a lot of him, Bill. But he learned to use a gun and he got to believe that he—he just couldn't miss." She paused and Bill saw tears gathering on her lashes. "He—had a quarrel—with a man who said something slighting about me, and he—Well, he—"

She stopped. The tears were running down her cheeks and she was biting her lip to keep from crying aloud.

Bill laid a gentle hand on her shoulder, patted her as he would a child. "I reckon I understand, Nancy. I'm terribly sorry. And I'll try to remember. Good night, dear."

He went out into the cool night. There was something in his throat that he couldn't swallow.

CHAPTER EIGHT

ILL WENT STRAIGHT from the Gospel tent to his cabin and
got out the stack of wanted notices to refresh his memory
with the contents of one of them. There was no mistake about it,
both picture and description fitted. The big man who had invited
him to come shooting on sight was Cherokee Smith, leader of a
band of outlaws who had participated in several train holdups.
Cherokee Smith had killed an express messenger and there was a
reward of $1,000 for him, dead or alive.

Bill put the notices away and went downtown again. He
moved about the streets, keeping a sharp lookout for Cherokee,
but did not enter the Frontier where the man was most likely
to be. He wasn't afraid of Cherokee, but his promise to Nancy
would be a severe handicap if the thing came to a shoot out. Bill
would have to try to disable while Cherokee would undoubtedly
shoot to kill.

He went into the Double Eagle, saw Wes Peters at the bar
and passed him without speaking. The councilman, Frank Cade,
was dealing faro at one of the tables and it occurred to Bill that
here might be the source of Monk Malone's information. None
of Malone's crowd patronized the Double Eagle, it being the
headquarters of the Cleanup Party, and affairs concerning the
reform movement were discussed rather openly. Fred Sivart was,
of course, a party to the secrets of the party and might have mentioned the candidacy of Tom Harrigan in the hearing of Cade.

Bill went out again. Noise from the Frontier came rolling
across the street in continuous waves, but still Bill did not go

into the place. If any fights broke out there were enough miners present to take care of themselves, and if they tore the joint apart it was all right with Bill.

He found the Lucky Tiger and went inside. It was the first time he had entered the place and he found it quite as dirty as was Ed Dillon, its owner. There was almost as much noise here as in the Frontier. The occupants were mostly roughs, probably crowded out of the Frontier by the miners. Girls and men kept going and coming through a doorway which led to another part of the building, and Bill guessed that Dillon's business was not confined to the sale of beer and whiskey. After taking a look around, Bill went out.

The combination marshal's office and jail was next door to the Lucky Tiger. Bill unlocked the door and went inside and lighted a lamp which stood on the battered desk. Besides the desk there were a cot, several straight-backed chairs, a gunrack holding an assortment of weapons, and a brass cuspidor. In the top desk drawer was a large key which Bill supposed fitted the cell locks, several pairs of handcuffs and their keys, and a plentiful supply of ammunition. The other drawers were crammed with accumulated wanted notices and circulars of various sorts.

Bill opened a door at the back of the room and, carrying the lamp, went into a dark corridor. There were two cells on each side of the passageway and a back door at its end which was bolted on the inside. Bill put out the light, locked up and continued his tour of the town.

There were a dozen saloons and they were all filled. Most of them carried gambling layouts and there were quite a few girls. Bill had never seen such a choice collection of roughs in one town, and his conviction that the Cleanup Party could never outvote them grew.

On his way uptown he entered the passageway between the Frontier and the barbershop and peered through a side window. He spotted Cherokee Smith standing with Smoke Rafferty near the doorway to Malone's office. If it hadn't been for his promise to Nancy he would have walked in and settled their differences without further ado, for Bill did not favor the postponement of necessary tasks no matter how disagreeable. In this case he would be under a constant strain until the thing was finished, and since there must be a showdown sooner or later he thought it the part of wisdom to have it now. But his promise to Nancy held him.

It was only ten o'clock but he decided to call it a day. The heck with Calder; let the roughs and the cowboys and the miners tear it apart and fight over the scraps. He went home and to bed.

Sunday again, and he slept late. There was never anything doing on Sunday mornings. He fed himself and his horse and sat for a while studying the wanted notices. He identified fully half a dozen more criminals, including three of the roughs who had been with Cherokee at the Gospel tent. He filed their names and descriptions away in his mind; when the time for settlement came the information would be useful. At ten o'clock he walked down to the Frontier and went inside. There was a single bartender and a swamper present and nobody else. The barman told him that Monk wanted to see him, and Bill wondered if Malone lived in that one room. He rapped on the door and went in. Monk was at his usual place behind the desk. He scowled at Bill. "About time you showed up. Tried to find you last night. Where you been keepin' yourself?"

"I've been around." Bill straddled a chair. "What's on your mind?"

"You. What in blazes you mean by pullin' that stunt at the tent? You wasn't hired to convert no heathen."

"You like to see your boys get rooked by a tinhorn?"

Monk's scowl became blacker. "I know you ain't that dumb. You oughta know why that shell game was planted there."

"All right, I know. So does everybody else. Suppose I say that I busted it up because it was a dumb play."

"Whadda you mean, dumb play?"

"Use your head. There were a lot of women in that tent. You might scare men away from the polls with stunts like that, but you just make the women mad and more determined than ever. I'll bet every woman who was in that tent will march her husband or son to the polls and make 'em vote for the Cleanup Party if she has to take a club to them. You're not as smart as I thought you were, Monk."

Malone glared at him and again Bill was impressed by the man's apparent helplessness. He didn't know how to answer; he must have ordered the disturbance yet he had no logical reason to justify it. He wet his thick lips and cleared his throat and the belligerence went out of him.

"Mebbe you're right; mebbe it wasn't so smart," he conceded at last. "But you sure got yourself in dutch by doin' what you did. Cherokee Smith's gunnin' for you." A malicious glint came into his eyes. "Mebbe that's why you was so hard to find last night."

"Could be. I have a rule never to shoot more than one man a day. Biff was my victim yesterday. I'll put Cherokee at the top of my list if it'll make you feel any better. Where does he hang out?"

"Got a place back of the livery corral. Three other fellers with him. If you want to die suddenlike, try bustin' in on 'em."

"Anything else you wanted to see me about?"

"Reckon not. But I was just thinkin'; what you done last night'll put you in more solid with the Cleanup bunch. Play up to 'em and keep your ears open; somebody might get confidential. And after this make sure about any setup you run into before you go bustin' it up."

Bill left the Frontier and walked up the street to the end of town. The Sunday morning service in the Gospel tent had just ended and people were coming out. There was quite a crowd and Bill was standing on the sidewalk watching them when Molly Sexton and Fred Sivart saw him. Molly said something to Fred and hurried to where he stood. Her deep blue eyes sparkled and her smile made dimples in her cheeks.

She said, "Bill, it seems as though I'm always apologizing to you. I'm sorry that I accused you of going over to the other side. Nancy told me about the six sinners you hauled up to the altar. It was marvelous! And what a story it'll make! I'm going to write it up for Thursday's paper; I think the Governor would enjoy reading about it."

Sivart joined them. He greeted Bill and smiled, but the smile did not reach his eyes. Bill thought, *The son-of-a-gun's jealous, and I don't blame him.* Sivart said, "That was a swell job you did last night, Bill. Maybe the Cleanup Party should arm themselves and escort all of Malone's bunch to the meetings. Rutherford might be able to talk a little brotherly love into their souls."

"I'm getting a lot of credit I don't deserve," Bill told them. "I marched them into the tent as a sort of joke. I thought it would be funny to make them listen, but they turned the joke on me by liking it. All except Cherokee Smith. Listening to a sermon was a humiliating experience for him."

"They tell me he's gunning for you."

"He sort of hinted that he didn't like me."

Quick alarm came into Molly's face and she put her hand on Bill's arm. "Bill, be careful. He's a dangerous man."

Bill grinned. "I like 'em thataway. I just grab 'em by an ankle and wave 'em—you know."

"I know you're going to grab the wrong ankle someday."

"We'd better be moving along, Molly," said Sivart. "We'll have to hurry if we want to get that ride in before dinner. So long, Bill."

They moved away and Bill's eyes followed them down the street. They made a handsome couple. Sivart's near six feet just the right height for her five feet five inches. Bill found himself wondering just how far Sivart's courtship had progressed.

The day passed uneventfully. Bill made no further effort to evade Cherokee Smith, deciding to leave their encounter to fate; but he did not meet the big man. Wes Peters, in accordance with their agreement, was in the Double Eagle that night, but Bill did not speak to him.

Monday came and went, a dull, uninteresting day. The free-drink sign had been removed from the Frontier and the miners in the gulch nursed a bad hang-over. Bill saw no sign of Cherokee Smith, who was probably nursing one of his own in the shack behind the livery corral. Bill inspected that shack from a safe distance, familiarizing himself with it as part of a plan which was maturing in his mind.

Tuesday likewise came and went. Hang-overs were gone and the town resumed its normal activities. Bill made his rounds and dropped in to see Judge Higby, the justice of the peace who garnered twenty-five per cent of all fines he imposed. He was a thin little man with a sour face and he complained at once of the lack of arrests since Bill had taken office. Bill assured him that he'd make up for lost time when he got the hang of the thing.

In the evening Bill took a position outside the Gospel tent, more, it must be confessed, to listen to Nancy's voice than to that of her father. He saw Molly in the *Clarion* office when he passed it, but did not disturb her chiefly because he could think of nothing to make the sparks fly. He saw Cherokee Smith twice, but both times the man disappeared without apparently having noticed Bill. Bill decided that either his ardor for a gun fight had cooled or he was waiting until chance favored him. The latter seemed the more likely.

Tom Harrigan did not come to town and Bill hoped that his supporters had convinced him that discretion was the better part of valor. On the other hand, Tom had had a severe scare and probably was nursing an even more severe hang-over.

Wednesday gave promise of no more excitement than the preceding three days had furnished, but when things started that evening they more than made up for the comparatively long stretch of peace and quiet. Bill was passing the *Clarion* office on his way downtown when Molly saw him and beckoned him in.

Her father was working on the press, preparing for the run of the paper which would come out on the morrow. Molly slapped the proof of an editorial before Bill and told him to read it. Her eyes were shining and her color was high.

Bill read. It was a blistering condemnation of Malone and his conduct of town affairs. It pulled no punches, accusing him flatly of harboring criminals for a price, of misappropriating funds and condoning crime. It accused him of planning John Turner's death and stated that Tom Harrigan had been marked for death but had been saved by some flaw in the plan.

Bill grinned at her and nodded his approval. "You finally got the old pick and shovel working. That ought to make them sit up and take notice. If Monk wins the election, which I believe he will, at least there should be some sort of an investigation."

"He isn't going to win. I'm betting the *Clarion* he won't."

"And I've covered that bet with a lifetime of service."

"You'll live to regret it. I'll put you at washing dishes and makings beds and scrubbing type and all sorts of disagreeable jobs."

"Looks like I'll have to vote for Malone in self-defense. Two or three times, if I can manage it." He saw a proof sheet lying on her desk and picked it up and read it. It was an article covering the affair at the Gospel tent. He said, "*Wow!* Listen to this: 'The offenders were escorted by Calder's new marshal into the tent and forced to attend the service and contribute liberally when the collection plate was passed. It would seem that our doughty marshal retains some respect for God even if he was appointed by Malone.' You sure worked the pick and shovel overtime there!"

"Like it?" asked Molly complacently. "I wrote it."

"I'd have never guessed," said Bill.

They chatted for a while, then Bill went out and down the street, keeping his eyes open for sight of Cherokee Smith. The eternal vigilance was wearying and he determined to end it one way or another. His course of action had been planned; he would shoot Cherokee in the leg and take the chance that the shock and paralyzing weakness would spoil the fellow's aim. Trying to stand on a broken leg is not conducive to good shooting. But he'd have to have good light for such fast and accurate work, so he went into the Frontier in the hope of finding Cherokee there.

He halted just within the doorway and looked around, and when he saw that Cherokee was not present, crossed to the bar. He took a place near its end where he could watch the door. Smoke Rafferty was standing at the faro table; he did not glance toward Bill and presently he sauntered out.

The outbreak came from the direction of the jail, a sudden fusillade of shots and a chorus of wild yells. Bill left the Frontier at a run and turned left. The fracas was at the Lucky Tiger. Men were streaming through the doorway, turning to shoot into the saloon when they reached the sidewalk. Inside, a loud voice was shouting, "I'm a son-of-a-gun from Sundown and I can lick any six *hombres* in this lousy town! Come on, you gun-slingin' marshal, and get polished off!"

Bill promptly obliged. He dived through the swinging doors and leaped to the left, his Colt in his hand. He glanced about quickly. The back-bar mirror was splintered and there was broken glass on the floor. The rear light had been shot out and was weeping oil onto the sawdust. There was but one man in sight, a rough called Big Bob Belcher, and Bill had read the notice which tagged him as wanted for stage robbery and murder. He was at the back of the room, surrounded with shadows.

If the fellow was a drunk as he sounded, his reflexes had not been affected, for even as Bill glimpsed him he leaped for the back door, not even loosing a shot at the marshal he had seemed so anxious to polish off. He yanked open the door and jumped into the dark alley and Bill sprinted in pursuit. It was time, he thought, that he and Judge Higby split a fine.

He halted by the piano which stood just to the left of the doorway, not foolish enough to bound into the darkness where the son-of-a gun from Sundown awaited him. He moved to the right of the doorway to peer out into the blackness, then leaped to the left side to look out at another angle. He was backed against the piano and some instinct caused him to turn his head. He was just in time to see the scowling, intent face of Cherokee Smith over the top of the piano; then Cherokee's gun barrel came down in a smashing blow and Bill sagged to the floor.

He was not completely out, but by the time he recovered his strength he was buried under a pile of human bodies and knew that his attackers must have been hidden in the saloon. The knowledge that he had been tricked lent him a savage strength, and he fought fiercely and silently. They were too many for him; the pile untangled and they yanked him to his feet. Every one of them had a bandanna mask over his face. Bill's gun was gone and half a dozen hands clutched his arms. When he was on his feet, more hands snatched his legs from under him and he was borne, kicking and struggling, into the alley.

The back door of the jail stood open; they carried him inside and tossed him into a cell. The door slammed and a key grated, then the whole crowd melted into the alley and he was alone with his rage.

He shouted and got no answer. He staggered to the door and shook the bars angrily but also futilely. He climbed on a bunk and shouted through the small window and still got no answer. At last, burning with rage and frustration, he sat down on the bunk and tried to compose himself.

Almost instantly he was on his feet again. From far up the street came a new outburst. There were shots and shouts and above them the sound of metal striking metal. The strokes were rhythmic punctuated by lesser crashes.

He heard boots thud on the wooden sidewalk as men ran up the street, drawn by the uproar. He sprang on the bunk and yelled some more, but his voice only added to the bedlam. He kept yelling until he was hoarse.

The sounds died away and silence fell. An ominous silence. He tried to yell again but the best he could manage was a feeble croak. He got down and paced about the cell, trying the bars again even while he realized the futility of it. The marshal was securely locked in his own jail while the devil danced on his doorstep.

And then he heard the thud of boots behind the jail and saw against the lighter blackness beyond the open rear door a man come bounding into the jail. The man called, "Bill!" and his voice was sharp with anxiety.

Bill managed to croak, "That you, Wes? Get me out of here. Key's in the top desk drawer."

Wes ran into the office, thumbing a match into flame as he did so. He returned within a minute and the key grated in the lock. Bill pushed open the door and leaped out. "What happened uptown?"

"Plenty. A crowd of roughs, masked with bandannas, busted into the *Clarion* office. They hustled Sexton and Molly out into the street, then gathered up all the papers and every scrap of proof and burned them in the alley. They busted the press into a thousand pieces with axes and scattered the type all over creation. They wrecked the place completely. As a newspaper, the *Clarion's* done."

"They hurt Molly?"

"No. But if she could have laid hands on a gun she'd sure enough have laid some of 'em low."

Bill leaned against the cell bars and started rolling a cigarette. No use to rush around and get all hot and bothered now. The damage was done and could not be repaired.

He told Wes what happened to him. "It was all planned, of course, and very neatly planned, too. The ruckus in the Lucky Tiger was staged to draw me inside where they could gang up on me and toss me in the jug where I'd be out of circulation. Once they had me locked up, they went in a bunch to the *Clarion* office and wrecked it. You see, Wes, the Sextons had changed their tactics. In tomorrow's paper there would have been a bold exposition of Malone and his protection racket. They were going to send copies of the paper to the Governor, the County Attorney, and the Sheriff. That was supposed to have been a secret, but in some way Malone got word of it. He just couldn't let a single copy of that paper remain, and he had to fix the plant so that it couldn't be printed over."

"Where'd he get the information?" demanded Wes.

"I don't know. There's a traitor in the outfit somewhere. Either that or Monk has somebody planted where he can overhear what's being planned. Frank Cade is a town councilman and he works for Sivart. The Double Eagle is a Cleanup hangout, and the boys talk. Malone may be getting his information from Cade."

"Could be," said Wes thoughtfully.

Bill dropped the cigarette butt and ground it beneath a heel. "Well, now that the horse is gone I'll take a look at the stable. You keep mum about turning me loose; I'm going to need you and I don't want anybody to know that we're working together."

Wes left by the rear door and Bill closed and bolted it after him. He left by the front way, locking the door and turning to his right toward the *Clarion* office. He was grim and fighting mad. From now on things were going to happen.

CHAPTER NINE

CALDER WAS CALMING DOWN again and Bill passed men on their way back from the scene of the excitement. In the patches of light where he was recognized they eyed him furtively and knowingly. His failure to show up when needed was in accordance with the best traditions of Malone marshals. He swore under under his breath. Molly Sexton and her friends would probably think that he had been a party to the outrage; that he had known of it and had deliberately remained away. Well, let them think what they would; he was being swayed too much by consideration of what their opinion might be.

He did his rage beneath an imperturbable expression and went up to the *Clarion* office. People stood on the sidewalk in front of the place staring curiously and whispering among themselves. The big glass window had been shattered and the door battered down; type was scattered all over the street. The interior was a wreck, the cast-iron wheels and frame of the press broken, the job press a mass of junk, the chairs and desks smashed and hacked. Neither Sexton nor his daughter were there.

Bill smoldered under more knowing glances and went to the Sexton home. There was a light inside and when he rapped on the door Molly answered. She gave him one hot look and tried to shut the door in his face, but he put a shoulder between door and frame and forced his way inside.

"You can't do this to me," he told her grimly. "I came to explain and you're going to listen."

"To more lies! I wouldn't believe you now if you were to swear to your story on a stack of Bibles a mile high. You've been working for Malone the whole while; it was you who kept him informed of our plans."

"You have a very short memory. How about the Gospel tent fire and the six-gun religion? I thought you had stopped doubting me."

"I was a fool. Not for doubting you, for letting you talk me out of it. The stunt at the tent on Saturday night was to get you back into our confidence. You put out the fire because you thought Nancy Rutherford was trapped. You find your amusement in burning orphaned children, not beautiful women."

"You're as cuckoo as a clock," he told her harshly.

"I was. I'm not any more. I'm cured. Tonight we needed you desperately. You were seen about town just a short time before. If you were really in sympathy with us you would have been on the job to protect us. You weren't."

"That's what I want to explain."

"I don't want your explanation. Never again can you talk me out of my opinion of you. Now go."

"If you'd just clamp the lid on and let me talk for a few minutes I can tell you all about what happened."

"If you haven't the decency to leave when I ask you to, you can tell it to the empty hall. I'm not going to listen."

She turned and ran up the stairs and Bill, after a moment, muttered an impatient "Damn!" and went out. He wasn't angry with her; he never could be angry with her. His actions had been so contradictory on so many occasions that the poor girl just didn't know where he really stood. News of their plans had reached Malone and he was the only stranger in the outfit; it was natural for her to distrust him.

He went on up the street. The Gospel tent was dark but the little one behind it where the Rutherfords lived had a light in it. Remembering Nancy's invitation to visit them, Bill rapped on the tent pole and presently the flap was flung back and he was looking at Nancy. She said, "Oh, it's you, Bill."

"Yes. Is your father's inside?"

"No; he's over at the Sextons." She came out and let the flap fall behind her. "Is there anything that I can do, Bill?"

"You just bet there is. I tried to talk to Molly but she ran out on me. She's got the idea now that I had something to do with the wrecking of the *Clarion* and wouldn't even give me a chance to explain why I didn't try to stop it."

"Molly's quick-tempered and given to snap judgments. Often she's wrong, and when she is, she's quick to admit it. Suppose you tell me about it."

He took her hand and led her over to the woodpile. She sat on the sawbuck and he squatted on his heels beside her. He told her just what had happened that night and offered the bump on his head in evidence.

"Molly'd probably say that I batted myself over the head to make my story convincing."

Her fingers on the sore spot were soft and caressing. "Poor Bill! You must forgive Molly; she's all unstrung after what happened. You can't really blame her for doubting you; you've teased her so much that she doesn't know when to believe you. But time is a great healer, Bill."

"I wish it would start healing. And talking about time, that election is rushing right up on us. Only eleven days, and Monk Malone is trumping your aces as fast as you lead them. You can't make a move without his knowing of it. He most certainly knew what would be in the paper tomorrow and that you were going to send copies to the authorities. Where does he get this information?"

"Bill, I can't even guess. We haven't been as careful as we might have. There are many people working with us and for us and we feel they are entitled to know our plans. We tell them in confidence or give them broad hints. They talk to others in the party. Somewhere along the line they are overheard."

"That's logical, Nancy, and it fits in with a hunch I have. One of the councilmen is named Frank Cade and he works for Fred Sivart at the Double Eagle. Wes Peters and the cowboys and miners go there and they naturally talk among themselves, and Fred knows everything that goes on where the Cleanup Party is concerned. Cade might make it his business to overhear. He could pass the news on to Malone at one of the council meetings. Monk may even have made him a councilman in order to have a spy in your camp."

Nancy sighed. "I'm afraid none of us ever thought of him. It's all very confusing, isn't it, Bill? But we'll win the election; I'm sure of it. The right must triumph."

He left her feeling quite a bit better, even though still convinced that right would run a poor second to might in the coming election. He went back to the Frontier, looked over the half doors at the crowd, then pushed through them and into the saloon. He had hoped to find Cherokee Smith, but the man was not there. He walked past the bar, pushed open the door to Monk's office and entered without bothering to knock. He had his right hand on the butt of the Colt he had taken from the weapon rack in the jail to replace the one which he had lost when he was attacked, and his gaze went first to the chair at the far side of the room.

Smoke Rafferty occupied it, and Bill's failure to knock caught him with his guard down. He had a glass of whiskey in his hand; he dropped it instantly and came to his feet, the hand darting for his gun; but Bill tilted up the swivel holster and said, "Hold it, Smoke!" and Rafferty arrested the motion. Bill said, "Sit down," and after a long moment Smoke sank slowly back into the chair.

Monk, behind the desk, said, "What's goin' on here! Bill, what's the idea of bustin' in thataway?"

Bill stepped over to one side of the desk and said, "Monk, I accused you of framing me when Biff tried so hard to get me. You alibied your way out of that and I believe you. Now don't try to tell me that knocking me out and chucking me in jail was Cherokee Smith's idea."

"Of course I ain't tellin' you that. The knockin' out was Cherokee's idea and I aim to give him hell for it when I meet up with him. But the rest of it was thought up by me. You wasn't to be hurt; you ain't hurt except for that little bust over the head. If I'd wanted to put you out of the way you can gamble you wouldn't be standin' here beefin' now."

Bill could readily believe that. "I'd sure like to know what your idea was."

"I'll tell you, Bill. You're a good marshal because you stand in with the Cleanup bunch. What would they have thought if you was runnin' around loose and hadn't showed up to help 'em tonight? They wouldn't be your friends no more. No, sir. So I figured it was best for you if a gang jumped you and put you where you couldn't interfere. They'll be stronger'n ever for you now. They'll figger that I didn't trust you enough to let you stay on the job. You go over and tell Fred Sivart how you was taken out of the play and he'll pass the word to the Cleanup bunch. You get it now?"

He was grinning, and Bill slowly lowered the muzzle of the Colt. It sounded logical enough except that Monk had never before bothered to worry about what the Cleanup Party might think of his marshal. But there was nothing Bill could do but accept Monk's explanation.

"Yeah, I guess I get it. But if you like me so much there's something you can do for me. Get my gun back. I've had it for quite a spell and I like it and am used to its feel."

Monk frowned. "Well, now, I don't know about that. How am I to know who got it or where it is?"

"Monk, you just about run Calder. Getting that gun back is a mighty little thing to ask in return for a busted head. You pass the word around and have that gun for me tomorrow."

"Well—all right." He spoke to Rafferty. "Smoke, take care of it."

Bill went home and put his sore head to bed.

Thursday and Friday passed without incident. Bill kept looking for Cherokee Smith and not finding him. He had a new incentive to find the fellow and Cherokee, knowing that Bill had recognized him before he struck, had an even greater one for keeping out of Bill's sight.

At noon Saturday the FREE DRINKS FOR MINERS sign was once more flying above the Frontier entrance. Just before suppertime Monk sent for Bill and Bill went into the office. Rafferty was not in the room.

Monk asked, "You get your gun back?"

"Yes. Barkeep gave it to me on Thursday. Much obliged."

"Forget it. Now listen. There's a play comin' up tonight and you ain't in on it. Mosey up to the Gospel tent and git yourself some religion."

"Is that an order?"

"That's an order. Better for you and better for us if you ain't down at this end of town."

Bill knew better than to ask Monk what was in the wind. He went out trying to guess what the play would be. Smoke Rafferty was at the end of the bar within two jumps of the office door and Bill slipped in beside him and ordered a drink. "Understand there's something on for tonight," he remarked casually.

"That's right. Maybe you also understand that you ain't in on it."

"I do. I'm to go to the Gospel tent and soak up some religion. But I am a little curious. I guess you'll handle whatever it is, won't you?"

"Keep guessin'."

That was all he could get out of Rafferty. He moved about the room listening to conversations in the hope of picking up some clue, but if the thing was generally known men weren't talking about it. He went to a restaurant for supper, still mulling over the matter. He came back down the street and went into the Double

Eagle. Tom Harrigan was at the bar and, as on the previous Saturday, kept glancing longingly across the street, mentally tasting the free liquor which was being dispensed to his mates. Bill's natural hunch was that some new plan to eliminate the Cleanup Party's candidate had been hatched.

He didn't know what to do about it. There was no chance now to get Molly or Nancy to work on Harrigan, and Tom would not listen to him in spite of his close call on the other occasion. It was doubtful if he would listen any more readily to Wes Peters or Fred Sivart. He was an obstinate Irishman.

Bill glanced about him. The crowd was slim, for it was still early and the miners were across the street. Frank Cade sat at the faro table practicing sleight of hand with a deck of cards; Sivart leaned against the end of the bar smoking a long thin cigar. Bill went down and took a place beside him.

He said in a low voice, "Tom Harrigan's getting restless and he has a short memory. He'll be crossing to the Frontier pretty soon and I got a tip that something's in the air. They may be planning to get him; can you talk him out of going over?"

"I doubt it. He's carrying just enough of a load to be mean and reckless. You got any ideas?"

"The only place I can think of where he'll be safe is in jail. But if I try to arrest him he'll put up a fight. Tell him that you got a straight tip that they're out to get him. Take him out the back way and down to the jail and don't let anybody see you if you can help it. I'll go down and open the back door. Take a quart of whiskey along to keep him company."

"Suppose I can't talk him into it?"

"Then feed him a loaded drink and when he's out we'll carry him down. I tell you, Fred, they're out to get him sure."

A voice behind them said, "Excuse me, gentlemen."

Bill swung around and saw Frank Cade standing at his elbow. Cade was looking at Sivart. "I'm out of cards, Fred. Got any in the office?"

"Sure. Come along and I'll get 'em for you. So long, Bill."

They went away leaving Bill frowning. How long had Cade been standing behind them and how much had he heard? Impossible to tell. There was only one thing to do. Bill moved down the bar to where Wes Peters was standing and brought the cowman a drink. While the barman was getting his change he said, "Stick around here and watch Frank Cade. Notice if he goes out or talks with anybody who leaves right afterward. See if he slips anybody a note. Don't slip up on this Wes."

Wes said, "Keno," and Bill downed his drink and moved away.

Sivart and Cade came from the office and Fred went to where Tom Harrigan stood, still stretching his neck toward the Frontier. Fred said something to him and they went into Sivart's office. Presently Fred came out and nodded slightly to Bill. Bill went out immediately.

He walked to the jail, unlocked the door and went in. He got the cell key from the desk and, still in darkness, went down the corridor to the back door. He unbolted this, went outside and stood in the shadows. Within five minutes he heard cautious footsteps and the shadowy forms of two men came into sight. One of them said in a low voice, "You there, Bill?" and Bill recognized the voice as belonging to Fred Sivart. He answered and led the way into the building.

Harrigan was protesting. "I don't like this, Fred. I'm not runnin' from any man alive."

"It's just a precaution you owe the Cleanup Party, Tom. Once you're elected you can go where you please and tell the whole crowd where to head in. I brought along a quart, and one of us will be seeing you later."

Still grumbling, Harrigan went into a cell. Bill locked the door after him, promised to drop in later and, after bolting the rear door, went out the front way with Sivart. He locked this door too and they separated at once. Bill stopped at the Frontier to look over the doors and saw Smoke Rafferty still standing at the end of the bar. He crossed to the Double Eagle, rolled a cigarette, felt in his pockets, then asked Wes for a match. Under cover of lighting up he whispered, "Anything doing?"

"Not a thing. Cade didn't go out, didn't slip any note. Talked to a couple fellers and one of 'em left. I know him, and think he's all right."

"Stick around and keep watching. I'm going up the street."

He went to the Gospel tent, entered it and sat down at the back. He wanted to be downtown where he could keep his finger on the pulse of things, but he had to play the game Malone's way to avoid suspicion. He was uneasy and a hunch kept whispering that all saw not right. He thought that possibly he had guessed wrong and that somebody other than Harrigan was in danger, might even then be lying with Smoke Rafferty's bullet in him. As soon as Rutherford pronounced the benediction he hurried out and went to the Frontier.

Everything was as it had been except that the noise and drunkenness had multiplied. Smoke Rafferty still stood at the bar. His uneasiness persisting, Bill crossed the street to the Double Eagle. Wes reported that Frank Cade had not left the room or handed anybody a note. He had spoken to several men and some of them had afterwards gone out, but Wes couldn't check their movements and watch Cade at the same time.

Fred Sivart came over with a newspaper-wrapped package. "Better take this down to Tom," he said. "I would have gone down myself but I forgot to get the jail key from you."

Bill took the package and went out. He walked to the jail, unlocked the door and went inside. It was very still. He got the cell key and went into the dark corridor. "Tom!" he called softly; then, when he got no answer, repeated sharply, "Tom!"

Still no answer. He thumbed a match into flame and held it up. Tom was lying on his back just inside the bars. He hadn't passed out, for his eyes were open and he was staring fixedly at the ceiling. His coat had fallen back and there was a dark stain on his flannel shirt.

And from the middle of that stain protruded the handle of a knife.

CHAPTER TEN

BILL SWORE worriedly and unlocked the cell door and went in. He knelt by the body in the darkness and felt for some sign of life, knowing as he did so that he would find none. He sat there on his heels, considering. He and Fred Sivart alone knew that Tom had been locked in the jail. Unless Fred and Tom had been seen on their way there and had been followed. Unless Frank Cade had overheard Bill and Fred talking and had managed to get word to Malone. The two unlesses bothered him.

The key. Malone in all probability had one to the front door, and Bill did not believe the cell had been unlocked. All the murderer had to do was slip into the dark corridor, whisper "Tom!" and Harrigan would have come close to the bars thinking his visitor was either Sivart or Bill. A quick thrust and it was done. This part was easy to figure.

The killer. That wasn't so easy. It might have been one of a dozen or more men, including Cherokee Smith. Not Rafferty. Rafferty was a gunman and stabbing would be beneath him. Just the same Bill would have to check on him and learn if he had left the Frontier while Bill was at the Gospel tent. There was no way of checking on Cherokee Smith, and to check on all the other key Malone men would be equally impossible.

Bill got up at last and went into the office to stand near the window and watch the street. He saw no movement out there and finally went to the back door, unbolted and opened it quietly, and stood there watching. So far as he could determine the jail was not under observation.

There was a lamp hanging from the ceiling and he lighted it. He scanned the corridor carefully and found that the killer had neglected to leave behind the slightest clue to his identity. The floor was of cement and there were no tracks. Bill went into the office, lighted the lamp and searched there. Nothing. Well, why should there be when all the killer had to do was walk in, stab Tom and walk out again?

He extinguished the light and sat down at the desk to study his problem in the darkness. If Sivart and Tom had succeeded in reaching the jail undetected, he could conceive only one source through which Monk had received his information. Frank Cade must have passed it on to one of the men he had spoken to and this man in turn had carried it to Malone. But it wasn't the one who had carried the message that Bill was primarily intersted in, it was the one who had plunged the knife into Tom's chest.

His thoughts gradually came around to his own situation. He was in a tough spot. He was the marshal and had the keys to the jail; the man who lay dead in the cell was the Cleanup Party's candidate for mayor; and the hue and cry he might raise over the finding of the body would be interpreted as pure bluff, akin to Biff Bang's charge on the roughs who were raiding the store. It was even possible that the miners, believing Bill guilty, might take the law into their own hands as had Wes Peters and his cowboys in the case of Sam Sneed. It wasn't a nice thought.

"We'll fix that right *pronto*," muttered Bill, and got up.

He worked rapidly. He went to the back door and opened it, stood listening and looking for a moment, then went into the cell, buttoned Harrigan's coat about him, picked him up carefully and held him cradled in his arms. This was doing it the hard way but he could not sling the body over his shoulder without getting blood on himself.

He carried the body out into the dark alley and walked toward the Frontier, pausing every dozen steps or so to peer about him and listen. Some distance from the jail and not more than fifty feet from the back door of the Frontier he lowered Tom to the ground, arranged him in a sprawling position, unbuttoned the coat and opened it. Then he hurried back to the jail.

He bolted the back door, lighted the corridor lamp and examined himself, the corridor and the cell for blood-stains He found none; Tom had fallen on his back and the knife had remained in the wound; what little blood there was had been soaked up by a flannel shirt.

Bill extinguished the light, left by the front door and hurried to the Double Eagle. Sivart was not in sight. Bill went to the office, opened the door and walked in. Fred was seated at his desk going over some accounts. He glanced up and asked, "How's he taking it?"

"He isn't. He's gone."

"Gone! Tom?" Sivart was thunderstruck. "You mean he's not in the cell? You're sure?"

"Positive. I even lighted the lamp in the corridor. The cell was unlocked and empty."

Sivart stared at him. "What could have happened to him?"

"He got out. Or somebody let him out. Are you sure nobody saw you taking him down there?"

"I was mighty careful. Of course I couldn't be positive. Harrigan kept talking." Sivart was disturbed.

"If you were seen going down there, Malone's men could have got him out. Malone probably has a key to the jail."

"I suppose he has. But I'm sure we weren't seen." His eyes went suddenly hard and he said, "You sure you haven't carted him off somewhere?"

"Why should I? I was the one who suggested putting him there."

"That's just what I was thinking."

Bill got it. He said sharply, "Listen, Fred; if I wanted to put Tom out of business I could have shot him last week or let Smoke Rafferty shoot him tonight."

"Maybe you didn't want him killed; maybe you just wanted him out of the way until after election. We couldn't run a missing man for mayor with any hope of electing him."

"You're as crazy as some other people I know. We'd better start looking for him."

"I don't think I'm crazy. Why do strangers come to Calder? Why should you be any different from the rest? I'm not pulling my punches, Bill; you tied up with Malone when you became town marshal, and now Tom Harrigan disappears from a cell to which you had the key. What do you want me to think?"

"I don't give a damn what you think. It's my hunch right now that we should be looking for Harrigan."

Fred got up from the desk and they went out into the barroom. Fred called Wes Peters over to them. "Tom Harrigan can't be found. I don't think he's over at the Frontier, but we'll see. Get your boys and comb the town; he may be asleep in an alley somewhere and we'd better find him before Malone's crowd does."

He's asleep in an alley, all right, thought Bill.

Bill went out with Sivart and they crossed the street and looked over the doors of the Frontier. Harrigan was not there. They went on down the street, looking in every saloon they came to. At the jail Sivart said, "I want to take a look for myself. Open up."

They went into the office and Bill lighted the lamp. He held it while Sivart went through the place. Fred entered the empty cell and examined it from wall to wall, then inspected the floor of the corridor. "Nothing," he said shortly. "No blood."

"Looks like he left under his own power," observed Bill.

They went out and resumed their search of stores and saloons. They had covered one side of the street and had worked up as far as Hollister's store on the other when Wes came hurrying to them. His face was grim. He said, "We found him. Layin' in the alley on the far side of the Frontier with a knife in his chest."

"Dead!" cried Sivart.

"As a mackerel."

"Near the Frontier, did you say?"

"Yes."

Sivart turned to Bill, his face distorted with anger. "You did it! You—" He stopped abruptly, seeming to pull himself together. "Let's take a look at him."

They went to the alley behind the Frontier where a small group of men had gathered. One of them had a lantern. Sivart knelt and made an examination, then got up and motioned to Bill to take over. "Ordinary skinning knife," Fred said briefly. "Dozens of them around."

Bill went through the motions of making an examination, then got up and said to Wes, "Take him over to Doc Bailey and tell Doc to fix him up for burial. Get in touch with some of the miners and find out if he had any relatives. I'll go down to his cabin and look things over." He handed Wes the deputy's badge he had in his pocket. "Pin this on; you're deputized. You and Doc take an inventory of what he has in his pockets."

He turned away and Sivart followed him to the street. There Fred halted him. He said, "We're going to have to drag this out into the open. Tom was murdered and we are the only two who knew where he was. We're going to have to tell about putting him in the cell."

"We are in a pig's eye," said Bill flatly. "To do that would be the same as accusing me of knifing him."

"That's just too bad for you, Bill. I'm coming clean."

"If you open your yap about locking him in the jail I'll deny it and toss the whole thing right in your lap."

"Go right ahead and try it. It'll be my word against yours. I'm a reputable citizen of Calder; you're a stranger and Malone's marshal. I don't think there's much doubt as to who they'll believe."

"They don't have to believe me; there are a few other reputable citizens they'll listen to. You were the last one seen with Tom while he was alive. He went into your office with you and nobody saw him come out. If they did, they saw him walking with you toward the jail and through the alley where he was found. Wes Peters saw you come out of your office without him; so did others. As for me, I was attending the Gospel service and some more reputable citizens can prove that, including Reverend Rutherford. Think that over, Fred, before you start spilling over about putting Tom in the jail."

There was a moment of silence, then Sivart said, "All right, damn you?" and stamped across the street and into the Double Eagle.

Bill got his horse and rode down into the gulch to Tom's cabin. It was unlocked and he went inside and lighted a lamp. He searched diligently but found nothing to show that Harrigan had any living relatives. He knew that most miners had hiding places for their gold and finally found a loose floor board beneath which were three buckskin pokes of dust. He took them with him rather than leave them for the prowlers who would undoubtedly search the shack.

He thought things over as he rode back to town. Somebody had slipped a very neat trick over on him and he didn't like it. The murder in this particular fashion could not have been planned in advance because no one had known that Tom would be confined in the jail; yet the killing had been carried out neatly, easily, and in such a way that suspicion must fall on Bill himself. He just couldn't believe that the slow-witted Malone was capable of hatching such a deft plot on such short notice. The old question asked itself again: If not Malone, who?

Wes found him in the Double Eagle and made his report. "We found the usual things in his pockets. No letters, a poke of dust, makin's and matches, silver watch, pocketknife, some change, pencil stub—just ordinary stuff. We made a list and Doc Bailey has it."

"Good enough. Are the boys still around?"

"I can round 'em up in a few minutes."

"Get them and meet me near the woodpile at the Gospel tent. Have them drift up there one at a time with their horses."

He saw Wes on his way, then crossed to the Frontier and went inside in the hope of hearing something which might give him a clue to the identity of Harrigan's murderer. He found only wonder and a mild consternation. Men discussed the matter in tones that reflected their complete surprise. He left the place no wiser than when he had entered. He mounted and rode up to the Gospel tent. Wes and his cowboys were waiting for him.

Bill said, "I'm going to arrest Cherokee Smith and his three buddies. There may be some shooting. You boys with me?"

"You're tootin' we are!" declared Wes, and the others echoed him.

Bill led the way along an alley to the livery corral and spotted the shack where Cherokee and his pals lived. It was lighted. At Bill's command they dismounted and led their horses, and he disposed them about the place and turned his horse over to Wes. "If I start shooting," he said tersely, "come running ready for work."

"You're not handlin' this alone," said Wes flatly.

"I don't reckon I'm that good; but I'll start the ball rolling. You'll be in at the finish, don't worry."

He moved away before Wes could question him, walking silently and swiftly toward the shack. He circled it at a safe distance, sizing it up, then moved quietly to a window and looked through the grimy pane.

There were four men in the room. Two of them were lying on thir bunks reading; a third sat in a chair sewing a patch on a shirt. Cherokee Smith sat in a tilted rocker with his feet on a table. He was rolling a cigarette and Bill noticed that he was wearing his gun.

Bill reasoned that the doors would be barred and that any tinkering with them would only alarm the occupants. He drew his Colt, made one swift slash at the pane, then thrust the weapon through the hole before the glass had ceased to tinkle. "Hold it!" he barked. "Hands up, everybody!"

Cherokee was already in action. With one heave he upset the chair, going over backwards. He did a somersault and came up on his knees with his gun out and blazing. It was quick work, wonderful coordination. A bullet nicked Bill's ear and glass bit at his face, and as he ducked sideways another slug kissed his cheek. He had Cherokee covered and could have shot him like a sitting duck, but he remembered his promise to Nancy and took desperate chances in order to keep it.

Cherokee was resting on his knees, supporting his weight on his left arm; Bill fired and the arm buckled like a matchstick and the man plunged forward on his face. Bill aimed deliberately and fired again and the gun flew from Cherokee's right hand as the bullet smashed his wrist. Bill heard Wes's yell and the thud of hoofs.

Horses slid to a stop before the shack and boots hit the ground. Wes appeared at Bill's side and the menace of his own .44 was added. The man who had been patching his shirt sat with hands raised, and Bill said to him, "Go over and open the door. And don't make any mistakes."

The man obeyed and the cowboys crowded into the room. Bill said to Wes, "I'm turning them over to you. Have the boys disarm them, tie their hands and herd them out of here. Saddle their horses, put them on them and take them to the Gospel tent where we met. I'll meet you there."

Wes had brought Bill's horse and it was standing over hanging rein. Bill mounted and rode to the livery stable. The councilman who looked and smelled like a horse was standing in the rear doorway of the stable holding a lantern. He recognized Bill and asked, "What's goin' on down there?"

"Just a little personal argument. Better keep away until they settle it."

Two of Malone's roughs came running through the stable and halted at sight of Bill. He gave them the same explanation and warned them to stay away. They hesitated, but here was silence around the shack now and the meddling marshal was right here beneath their eyes. They finally turned back. Bill waited five minutes or so more, talking with Pete Stacy, then said so long in a casual voice and rode to the Gospel tent.

The cowboys and their prisoners were waiting for him. Cherokee's wounds had been attended to, but he was in great pain.

Bill asked Wes, "Is that log stable strong enough to hold them?"

"It sure is."

"Then let's head for it."

They rode slowly, for Cherokee Smith was in agony, and it took them two hours to make the trip to the Turner ranch. They put the prisoners into the log stable, barred the doors and posted two guards to watch the place. Wes had spiked pieces of two-by-fours over the small window, evidently guessing to what purpose Bill intended the structure.

Bill went into the bunkhouse with them. Wes lighted the hanging lamp and they seated themselves at the table. Bill got out a wanted notice and spread it for them so see. "Cherokee Smith is wanted for train robbery and murder. I have notices for the other three also. In the morning, take them to the county seat and turn them over to the sheriff. Tell him to grill them on Harrigan's death and Malone's protection racket. What reward you collect you can split among you."

Wes said, "If there's any reward comin', my share goes to Mrs. Turner and the kids."

"That goes for me, too," quietly said one of the cowboys. The others stated their intention to turn their shares over, too.

Bill said, "That's swell. And this'll mean four less votes for Malone. Hurry back, for there'll be more shrinkage before we get through. Find me a sheet of paper and an envelope, Wes; I want to write a note to the sheriff."

He wrote swiftly for a few minutes, then folded the paper and sealed it inside the envelope and gave it to Wes.

"All this is strictly on the quiet," he told them impressively. "Don't mention what we've done to a soul, unless you have to explain to Mrs. Turner. If you do, swear her to secrecy. We're playing a dangerous game, boys, and we mustn't make a slip. The whole cleanup of Calder, as well as your lives, may depend upon your discretion."

"We're tight as clams," said Wes. "But, Bill, it ain't fair that we have all the reward. You're the one who's takin' the chances and doin' most of the work. You oughta get a cut yourself."

"Think so? Well, let's see. What do you figure should be my share? How about twenty-five per cent? That's what I get from Malone."

Wes blinked but answered promptly enough. "Whatever you say, Bill. You're entitled to all of it, as far as I'm concerned."

Bill grinned. "All right. Let's call it twenty-five per cent. But I can't let you fellers get ahead of me. I'm donating my share to Mrs. Turner and the kids, too."

Their faces brightened. Wes said, "Bill, you're sure a good man."

"I'm afraid everybody doesn't agree with you," he answered, thinking of Molly.

"Malone won't think so, if he ever finds out what you've done."

Bill said thoughtfully, "I've wondered a lot about Malone. I'm still wondering."

"Wonderin' what?" asked Wes.

"Wondering if he's really the snake in the grass that we're looking for. Sometimes I doubt it."

CHAPTER ELEVEN

I T WAS LONG after midnight when Bill returned to Calder, and he went at once to the Frontier. The noise, which had abated when the stunned miners learned of Harrigan's death, had resumed its normal volume, liberal shots of whiskey and the notes from the two-piece orchestra contributing to their recovery from the shock.

The miners guessed that Harrigan's death had come at the hands of one of Malone's roughs, but the murder did not cause the stir it would have had they known of Tom's candidacy. Quarrels that resulted in killings were common enough, and if this was a personal affair between Tom and one of the Malone outfit, it was Tom's hard luck that he had come out second best.

Smoke Rafferty, still at the end of the bar, saw Bill enter and jerked his head toward Malone's office. Bill went in, and at sight of him Monk's heavy face wrinkled in a scowl. "Where in blazes you been?"

Bill sat down and said coldly, "Investigating the murder of Tom Harrigan and taking care of things in general."

"You sure can make yourself hard to find when I want you. What was Harrigan doin' layin' in the alley so close to my place?"

"Well, he wasn't taking a nap."

"Did you knife him?"

"I was up at the Gospel tent absorbing religion when it happened. You sent me there. Remember?"

"If you didn't do it, who did?"

"You ought to know."

"Damn you, feller! You keep a civil tongue in your mouth. If I knew who killed him I wouldn't be wastin' time askin' you."

Bill was forced to agree that this was quite true. Monk knew that Harrigan had been slated for death the preceding Saturday night and Monk knew that Bill knew. There was no reason for evasion between them on this point. An idea that was gradually taking shape in Bill's mind grew stronger, but he decided to string it out a bit longer.

He leaned forward and stuck out his chin and said, "Monk, it's time you quit treating me like an idiot. You had Tom framed last week and you told me yourself there was something in the wind tonight. You sent me up to the tent to keep me out of it. I come back downtown to find that Harrigan was stabbed to death in the alley within fifty feet of the Frontier and you try to pull the bluff that you don't know a thing about it. How dumb do you think I am?"

Monk said heatedly, "I don't think you're dumb at all; I think you're a pretty smart *hombre*. But I'm tellin' you I don't know any more about who stuck that knife in Tom than the man in the moon. Our setup was entirely different and it didn't come off because Tom never showed up at the Frontier. Only way I can figger his killin' is that somebody bumped him off for his wad."

"You're wrong there. Tom wasn't knifed for his money. We found a poke of gold on him. Wes Peters and Doc Bailey took an inventory of his stuff and nothing was missing."

Monk grunted. "You think if one of my boys done it he'd leave a poke of gold on the feller?"

"He would if you ordered him to. It would be a smart play, Monk, the surest way of convincing people that you *didn't* have it done."

"They tell me you went through Harrigan's cabin down at the gulch. You find anything?"

"Not a thing to show Tom had any relatives. There was a loose floor board and under it I found this." He drew a poke of gold from his pocket. The other two he had left at the Turner ranch; this he had brought along for bait.

Monk said, "Good for you! Hand it over."

"Why should I?"

"I'm mayor, ain't I?"

"And I'm marshal, kicking in with half my salary and supposed to make it up on gravy from the side."

"You get your share of the fines; this dust is somethin' else again. I'll take charge of it."

"More sinews of war for the organization, huh?"

"Whadda you think? Tom didn't leave no relatives."

Bill weighed the gold in his hand. "About three hundred dollars, I should say." He put the poke in his lap, got out a pencil and tore a sheet of paper from a tablet on Monk's desk. He wrote:

Received of Calder's marshal, one poke of gold containing about three hundred dollars, property of Tom Harrigan, deceased, to be used by the organization.

He pushed it across the desk and said, "Put your John Hancock to that and the money's yours."

Monk read it and pushed it back. "I ain't signin' nothin'. You hand over that dust."

Bill put the poke back into his pocket. "Not without that paper to protect me. I'm in bad enough as it is. I'm going to take the blame for Tom's death and you know it. He was the Cleanup Party's candidate and I'm one of the original seven who knew it. I've got to be in the clear with that gold, for some of the miners would know he had it. You sign that receipt for it or I'll turn it over to Reverend Rutherford."

Monk stared at him angrily, then drew the paper toward him and re-read it. "What's this 'deceased'? Tom wasn't sick."

"That's the lawyers' words meaning that he's ceased to be. Don't make any difference; just makes it sound better."

Monk scratched out "deceased" and wrote "dead" in its place, then scrawled his signature. Bill said much obliged, took the paper and handed over the gold. He did not let his face show the elation he felt. Monk had taken the bait; he had missed the significant part of the receipt, the part which acknowledged over his signature that the gold was to be used for the "organization." This statement was definite proof that an organization did exist.

Bill left with his opinion of Malone even lower than it had been before. The organization was reputed to be a smart one; either it was greatly overrated or its brains were being furnished by somebody other than Malone. He remembered Frank Cade. Cade was quiet and unobtrusive, but he seemed to be intelligent, he spoke good English, and it could have been he who had printed the placard which had been nailed on the front of the store.

Bill hung around town keeping in contact with four men he had selected from among those who were described on his wanted notices. Two of them were in the Frontier, and when they left he followed them to the shack they shared. One of the remaining two was in the Lucky Tiger, and the fourth was in a joint called the Gold Standard. He followed them home in turn, locating the places where they lived in his mind for future reference. It was three o'clock when he finally turned in.

He awoke the next morning at the usual time, realized that it was Sunday and turned over and went back to sleep. When he awoke again it was nearly nine. He got up, fed his horse and then himself, put on a clean shirt and scarf and walked up to the Gospel tent. He stood near the entrance watching the people who entered. He got some cold looks from the women and no recognition whatever from the men. Molly passed him, walking between her father and Fred Sivart. They ignored him when he raised his hat, but he saw the angry color in Molly's cheeks and the smoldering fire in her eyes.

He heard the creak of wheels and turned his head and saw a spring wagon coming up the street. In it was a long wooden box and its driver was Doc Bailey, dressed in a black frock coat and a beaver hat. Four men sat on the box, looking gloomy. They were burying Tom Harrigan in a hurry.

The wagon drew up outside the tent, the box was unloaded and carried inside by the four men. Bill crossed to the woodpile and seated himself on the sawbuck. He sat there for an hour smoking and listening to the sad strains of the organ and the deep voice of Reverend Rutherford.

The service ended, the four men came out with the box and placed it in the wagon, then climbed aboard themselves. Doc Bailey got on the seat, said "Giddap" to the team and the vehicle moved slowly down the street. Rutherford and Nancy came out, followed by Sivart and Molly and the rest of the congregation. They moved in a grave procession toward Boot Hill. Bill rolled another cigarette and composed himself for another wait.

Rutherford and Nancy returned alone and were about to enter their quarters when Nancy saw Bill. She spoke to her father and the two of them came over to him. He got up and removed his hat and Rutherford said, "Good morning, Bill. We haven't seen you lately. Did you attend the funeral?"

"No, sir. Tom was practically a stranger to me, and probably all the people in that tent think I had something to do with his death."

"I don't think that," said Nancy. "If they could only understand that you took the job of marshal to help us, they wouldn't either."

"Do you really believe that, Nancy?"

"Of course, I do. You saved Tom Harrigan from being shot by Marshal Bang, I'm sure of it. You would have saved the *Clarion*, too, but Malone had you beaten up and locked in the jail. And last night they took advantage of your being at the service to kill Mr. Harrigan. I know you were here, for I saw you."

Her faith touched Bill. He said after a moment, "If you'd like to listen I'll tell you what really happened last night."

"We'd like to know, Bill," said Rutherford. "Come into the tent."

He went with them into their living quarters. It was cramped but tidy. Nancy indicated a little curtained-off corner with a faint smile. "My boudoir, Bill. Won't you sit down?"

Her boudoir! A lovely young girl like Nancy, with all the love of a woman for nice surroundings, and she cooped herself up in a little six-by-eight cubbyhole. Only one who sincerely believed in the cause for which she fought could be happy and content in such surroundings. His respect for her increased.

He told them of his conversation with Malone which led him to believe that Harrigan was in danger and of the plan he and Fred Sivart had made in an effort to save Tom. He even told them of his moving the body. "It looked as though I was slated to take the blame, and I couldn't do that. I had to be free to see this thing through." He observed them gravely. "You see, I don't believe it's Malone who's behind the wicked element in this town. I don't think he's smart enough."

They were frankly surprised. Rutherford said, "I thought it was plain that Malone manages the organization. All the evidence we have points to it."

"The evidence points to Malone as the one who sees to the execution of the plans; I don't think you have any evidence that he conceives them. Several times when a quick decision was needed Malone has stalled as though he had to consult somebody else before making his move. Last night he sent for me and wanted to know who had killed Harrigan. He wasn't bluffing; he was angry and baffled. Monk isn't subtle; you can read him like a printed page. He told me that the plan they had hatched to get Harrigan didn't mature because Tom didn't show up at the Frontier.

"My hunch is that the stabbing was arranged for on the spur of the moment, after the unknown leader of the outfit learned of our plan to lock Tom in the jail. This person, whoever it is, had no opportunity to contact Monk and tip him off as to the change in the arrangements, and Monk was all up in the air about it."

Rutherford was frowning in concentration. "It could be so," he admitted at last. "I never dreamed of any other leader than Malone. It's an alarming situation, not knowing who this enemy of ours is. Who in Calder would be astute enough to pull all the strings and still keep in the background?"

"I've thought of one who could, and I'm keeping an eye on him. What do you know about Frank Cade?"

"Cade? Why, nothing much except that he works for Fred."

"That's one reason why he might be our man. Nobody seems to know much about him. He's quiet and unobtrusive, but he's smart and educated. On the day Sam Sneed shot from the roof of the Frontier and killed John Turner, a signal was given him by somebody in the crowd. I was watching you, and I saw a hand behind you raised over the heads of the crowd to wave a white handkerchief. The shot followed at once. The arm was in a black sleeve and Cade wears a black coat.

"Then take that placard that was nailed on Hollister's store the day it was raided. It was neatly printed and all the words were properly spelled. It wasn't Monk Malone's work. Finally, Cade's working for Sivart gives him the chance to overhear what the Cleanup people are planning, and his job as councilman lets him contact Malone almost at will. He was standing right behind Fred and me when we made our plan and could have overheard it."

Rutherford shook his head. "It's all very bewildering. I was sure—"

"So was I at first; but Malone just don't fit. Last night when I realized that Cade might have heard Fred and me talking, I had Wes Peters watch the man. Cade spoke to several men who later left the Double Eagle. One of them could have done the job, or ordered one of their knifemen to do it. Cade would have a key to the jail if he's back of Malone. It would have been easy."

Rutherford said grimly, "We must warn Fred about him."

"Don't do it," said Bill promptly. "Don't mention what I've told you to a soul. Not even to the Sextons. I want to handle this my own way; let them go on suspecting Malone. I've succeeded in getting on the inside where I wanted to be; I can't trust even my own brother." He added with a smile, "Which should show you folks just where you stand with me."

"We do appreciate your confidence, Bill," said Nancy warmly. "And we won't tell a soul. Promise, Father."

Rutherford promised.

Bill said, "Thanks. Who are you going to run in Harrigan's place?"

There was an embarrassed silence, and Rutherford and Nancy exchanged worried glances. Nancy said, "Bill, we just can't tell you. We've passed our word not to tell anybody. But please understand that Father and I trust you entirely; it's just that we can't tell without breaking our word."

"It's just as well if I don't know. If anything happens to the new candidate you'll at least know that I wasn't the informer. The only reason that I wanted to know was so that I could keep an eye on him."

"I wish we could tell you," said Rutherford earnestly. "I'd feel better if I knew that you were looking after him. If anything happened to him our last hope would be gone, and we simply must win this election."

They urged him to stay to dinner but Bill declined, feeling that his presence as a guest might cause them embarrassment should it become known to their coworkers; but he left them with the warm feeling that he had found that rarest of treasures, real friends.

Toward evening things started humming again, with the free-drink sign still flaunting itself above the Frontier entrance. There was much talk but no trouble of any kind. Bill had found that Calder's outbreaks came at intervals, like tropical storms. with peaceful interludes intervening.

That night he followed four more wanted men to their homes, then got out the wanted notices and checked them once more. Again the notice describing Al Travis caught his attention, and once more he studied it. Age, 28. That would fit Frank Cade. Height, five feet eleven inches. Cade again. Weight, 175. A little on the heavy side, but within ten pounds. Color of hair, blonde. Cade's hair was black, but hair can be dyed. Color of eyes, blue. He'd have to check that. He knew that Cade's eyes were dark, but whether dark blue or black he couldn't be sure. There remained the six-inch knife scar on the chest; no way of checking that short of stripping the man.

Wes and his cowboys were not in town that night, nor did Bill expect them to be. It would take a day to travel to the county seat and another to return. Monday came and dragged by, and that evening Wes came into the Double Eagle. Bill caught his eye, flashed him a significant look and went out. Wes followed and caught up with Bill in a dark spot where Borden awaited him. He reported that the sheriff had welcomed them with open arms and their prisoners with open cells. A doctor had worked on Cherokee, and the man had been grilled. No dice. The other three were identified and two of them carried rewards for their apprehension. The reward would be forwarded to Mrs. Turner. One of them had admitted paying for protection but claimed that the collector of the tribute had been Marshal Bang.

"Biff may have collected it," said Bill, "but he didn't keep it. Did the sheriff say anything about my note?"

"Looked right pleased when he read it and said he'd do what you asked—whatever that was."

"I'll tell you someday, Wes. How'd you like to round up another bunch of bad men tonight and collect some more reward money for Mrs. Turner?"

"Bill, does a hoss like oats? The boys are out at the ranch but I can get 'em in a hurry."

"Suppose you get them and meet me at the Gospel tent around midnight."

The second raid was easy. Two of the men Bill had selected for capture lived together, the other two lived alone. They tackled the pair first. Two cowboys were assigned to catch up and saddle their horses; the other three were posted outside the house to prevent interruption. The door was not barred; Bill and Wes walked into the cabin, yanked the awakened men out of their bunks, lighted a lamp and set it in a corner where it would not show too plainly and waited while the men dressed. Bill had brought handcuffs from the jail and these were snapped about their wrists and they were taken outside and turned over to two of the cowboys. They were roped on their horses and sent with the two guards to the Turner ranch.

At the next stop, one man caught up and saddled while two watched. Again Wes and Bill walked in and brought out a prisoner. He was tied to his saddle and sent with two of the cowboys to the ranch for safekeeping.

The door of the third was locked, but Bill's cautious knock brought the occupant to the door with a whispered, "Who is it?"

"The marhsal," said Bill softly. Monk has a job for you. Open up."

The fellow let Bill in without further ado, and Bill stuck his .44 into the man's midriff while Wes came in and lighted a lamp. They made the man dress and go with them.

"Well, this is gettin' easier right along," said Wes cheerfully.

"We're improving with practice," Bill told him. "You and your remaining man can take him over. Here are the four wanted notices. Three of them carry rewards and something may have been offered for the fourth by this time. Take 'em to the county seat tomorrow and tell the sheriff to put them through the mill. Four of you ought to be enough for the trip; that'll leave two to take care of the ranch chores."

Wes was very happy about the way things were going. "We don't worry about no ranch chores. We told Mrs. Turner about it and she's with us a hundred and fifty per cent. Said she and the kids could run the place while we're gone. Bill, I'm beginnin' to find out that this is fun. Four more votes lost to Malone! Keep this up and the Cleanup Party can't help but win. And Mrs. Turner can give up cow ranchin' and take to snatchin' outlaws. More money in it."

"I reckon that all the rewards for all the criminals in the world wouldn't make up for John's loss."

"You're right," agreed Wes soberly. "But you sure have done your bit to pay her back."

"I'm getting to be a regular fanatic about righteousness," grinned Bill. "I been hanging around the Gospel tent too much."

CHAPTER TWELVE

Tuesday was outwardly quiet; inwardly things were beginning to simmer. Bill had hardly gone into the Frontier when Smoke Rafferty came from Malone's office and told him Monk wanted to see him. The dandified gunman was tight-lipped and bright-eyed and Bill was immediately on guard. He had anticipated the interview and was ready for it. When he entered the office he remained standing until Rafferty, at a sign from Monk, sat down; then he took a chair where he could watch both men.

Monk said abruptly, "Where's Cherokee Smith?"

"I know where I wish he was. I still owe him for batting me over the head down at the Lucky Tiger."

"I know all about that; I'm askin' you where he is."

"You'll have to ask somebody else. If you find out, let me know; I've been looking for him myself."

Malone eyed him steadily. "Saturday night Pete Stacy said there was some shootin' down at Cherokee's shack. Stacy seen you around there. Sunday mornin' Cherokee and his three pals turned up missin'."

"Lots of things happened Saturday, including the stabbing of Harrigan."

"Every time I ask you somethin' you talk all around the subject," complained Malone. "I want straight talk and no dodgin'. Where's Cherokee?"

"What do you want me to say—that I walked into Cherokee's place, shot all four of them, hid the bodies somewhere and then swapped jokes with Stacy?"

"Damn you, feller! I warned you about makin' a monkey of me!"

"You're making a monkey of yourself. You told me it was sudden death to walk in on those four; now you're accusing me of doing just that and getting away with it."

"Mebbe you tricked 'em," said Monk darkly. "I'm beginnin' to think you're pretty slick thataway."

"Use your head, Monk. I had every right to rub Cherokee out and I'd have done it if we'd met face to face; but I wouldn't be foolish enough to try to shoot it out with all four of them. I'll admit I'm good, but not that good. And what would I have done with them after I shot them?"

"I dunno; I sure don't." The harassed look was on Malone's face again. "Things are happenin' around here that never happened before, and they didn't start happenin' until you showed up in Calder. I knew that you and Cherokee was feudin' and when he didn't show up I thought of you right off."

"That'd be natural enough if it was only Cherokee who showed up missing, but you tell me his three pals are gone, too. Did they take their horses?"

"The hosses are gone, yeah."

"Looks like they cleared out then, don't it? I sure hope so. If the other three were anything like Cherokee I won't miss them. That all you wanted to see me about?"

"No. You figgered out yet who killed Harrigan?"

Bill looked pained. "Monk, I had that figgered out from the start. He's the Cleanup Party candidate and one of the boys removed him from circulation just like Sam Sneed removed Turner."

"I told you I didn't know a thing about it!"

Bill shrugged. "That could be. Maybe one of your boys killed him as a favor to you and is too modest to say so. Say! Maybe it was Cherokee who did it!"

"Aw, get the hell outa here!"

Bill backed out and Rafferty got up and followed him. At the bar Rafferty said, "I ain't satisfied with your tale, feller. I got a hunch you're playin' Malone for a sucker. I got another hunch that you put somethin' over on Cherokee and his boys. Cherokee's another friend of mine. That makes two of my friends you got to account for."

"There's just one of your friends that I'll account for," Bill told him coldly. "And that's the best friend you got in this world—yourself."

"You and how many others?" sneered Rafferty.

"After shooting it out with Cherokee and his boys and coming back to talk about it, how many others do you think I need?"

Evidently Rafferty wasn't sure about that for he said nothing more.

When Bill walked up the street he was surprised to find that new glass had been put in the *Clarion* office window, a new door hung, and that the wreckage had been cleaned up. Furthermore, Molly Sexton was seated at her damaged desk sorting large type from a pile before her. He opened the door and went in and leaned against the desk. He said, "Is our star reporter still mad, or has her better judgment prevailed?"

She observed him coldly. "No, I'm not mad. I've just decided that since I have nothing to do with other Malone hirelings I should have nothing to do with his marshal."

"Still think I'm the talebearer, huh?"

"More so than ever, since Saturday night."

"I gather from that that Fred told you of our plan to put Tom in storage and the way it kicked back in our faces. Did he mention Frank Cade to you?"

"What has Frank Cade got to do with it?"

"He may have everything to do with it. He was standing behind us when we talked the thing over. He might have heard what we were saying. And be sure to peddle that information around if you want to make things tough for me, which you probably do."

Flame leaped into her eyes and the pink rose in her cheeks. "I can keep my own counsel on occasion. You should know that, Mr. *Borden*." She went on heatedly, "You're very clever about clouding the issue. Now you're dragging in a man who simply works for Fred in order to divert my thoughts from what you were doing on Saturday night. You're a Malone man and you have the key to the jail. Also you knew that Tom was our candidate. If you wanted to you could have taken him back to that place where they found him and—and—"

"Stuck him like a pig. Go ahead; don't be afraid of a little gore in the conversation. I'm a Malone hireling, you know; you won't shock me. And you could be right except for one thing. I was being a good Christian when Tom was killed. I was up at the Gospel tent listening to Rutherford's sermon. Malone himself sent me up there. I think he wanted to get me out of the way but knew he couldn't work the same stunt he used the night the *Clarion* was wrecked."

Her eyes widened. "What stunt was that?"

"The one I called at your house to tell you about. Remember? The night you told me to tell it to the walls. You didn't want to hear about it then, you can't possibly want to hear about it now."

Molly tossed her dark curls. "You don't have to tell me; I'm not particularly interested in hearing about it."

"That's good, for I'm not particularly anxious to tell you. You'd probably say I was lying. Well, as Nancy told me, time is a great healer. You'll sure need a lot of it before you get well. Good day, Miss Sexton."

He started for the door and she called, "Bill!" He turned his head and lifted an eyebrow and she asked, "Does Nancy know—about that stunt?"

"Certainly she does. There's a girl right after my own heart. She believes in me and trusts me. I told her about it right away and she even felt the lump on my head."

He opened the door and she called again, "Bill! What lump?"

He turned again and spoke from the doorway. "Thought you didn't want to know?"

"But—but I do!"

"Sorry. Molly, you're a nice gal and for some strange reason I like you; but I've learned my lesson. I keep confidences strictly for those who trust me."

He went out and closed the door. His eyes were twinkling and he was chuckling again. Tormenting Molly was fun. He crossed the street and stood in a passageway between two buildings, and presently he saw Molly come out of the *Clarion* office and hurry toward the Gospel tent. He chuckled again and went to his cabin.

That night when he was in the Frontier, Rafferty slipped up to the bar beside him and said, "Four more of our fellers are missin'. You wouldn't know anything about it, would you?"

"Did they take their horses?"

"Yeah."

"Then why ask me? You're getting as bad as Monk. When I get through with fellers they don't need horses, they need hearses."

"Somethin' tells me you're fixin' to ride in one of them things yourself."

"I might try it. I never rode in one. I'll tell you how I enjoyed it when we meet outside the pearly gates."

He went out to make his rounds of the town, and it wasn't very long before he realized that he was being followed. His shadower kept far enough away from him to avoid being recognized, and Bill pretended to be unaware of his presence. He believed he could shake the fellow whenever he pleased.

Wednesday was uneventful too, but the same air of tension persisted. Wes showed up in the Double Eagle that night and Bill had a drink with him and designated a meeting place, setting the time for half an hour later. He went out, noticed a man detach himself from the shadows to follow him, and set about losing him.

It wasn't very difficult. As town marshal Bill could go just about where he pleased. He could enter a place by the front door and leave by the rear one, and this is just what he did, still pretending not to know that he was being followed. When he had thrown the fellow off the track, he went to the meeting place to find Wes waiting for him.

Wes gave his report. The prisoners had been safely delivered and had been grilled by the sheriff. Apparently they knew nothing of Harrigan's death. One had confessed that he had paid Monk five hundred dollars for protection. He seemed bitter because Monk had allowed him to be taken, and put his statement in writing. They were gradually getting the goods on Malone.

"Got another bunch spotted for cuttin' out?" asked Wes eagerly.

"Not tonight. I'm being shadowed and we mustn't get caught at this. Monk is worried and Smoke Rafferty's getting the jitters in his trigger finger. If we lay off for a few days they may pull off the trailer. We'll get some lined up for Sunday night. You can take them to the county seat on Monday and get back to Calder in time to vote on Tuesday."

On Thursday morning he met Molly on the street. She was distributing printed sheets to places of business and handed him one to read. It consisted of a single paragraph printed in large type on a single sheet of paper.

"How'd you manage to get this out?" he asked.

"We found an undamaged frame and collected the type from the street. We set it up, ran an inked roller over the type and printed the sheets one at a time. Go ahead and read it."

Bill did so. It said:

The Malone machine is responsible for the deaths of John Turner and Tom Harrigan This is common knowledge. If we want a decent town and an honest administration we must destroy that machine. If you do your duty and vote for the Cleanup Party's candidate the machine is done.

For his own protection our candidate's name will not be announced until election day.

"That's the stuff!" Bill approved. "Now you're really putting on the pressure."

"I'm glad you think so, Bill. We're going to follow up with a new sheet every day between now and Tuesday. We're going to see that every decent citizen sees them, and you're going to owe me that lifetime of service in spite of anything Monk Malone can do."

"You haven't much to lose, with the *Clarion* down to a single frame, some secondhand type and an ink roller; but the bet's still on."

"If you win you'll be paid the equivalent in some form," she told him proudly. "The *Clarion* doesn't welch on its bets. And, Bill—" She hesitated and the pink crept into her cheeks. "I talked with Nancy. She told me—what you would have told me if I hadn't been too stubborn to listen. Bill, I—I guess I'm sorry again."

"Think nothing of it," he said cheerfully. "I wouldn't feel natural if you didn't doubt me at least twice a week. Still keeping the name of your candidate a dark secret, I see."

She said yes and looked doubtful. He hurriedly added, "Don't tell me; you'll regret it later."

She shifted the bundle of papers to her other arm and he caught sight of something which for some reason hit him like a blow beneath the belt. He said, "What's that on your finger?"

"That? Just a ring."

"An engagement ring?"

"Yes."

"Fred Sivart, I reckon. Have you set the date?"

She looked at him for a moment, seemed about to speak, then evidently changed her mind. She lowered her eyes and said, "Not yet. It's quite tentative."

"Well, I reckon you know you have my best wishes for all the luck and happiness in the world." He forced a grin. "I just got to win that bet now; I sure don't want to wash dishes and make beds for Fred Sivart. So long."

His feet dragged a bit as he went up the street. So she was going to marry Fred. Well, why not? No reason for him to be bothered, unless it was by the thought that he would not have her to torment any more. A fellow doesn't feel free to exchange banter with another man's wife. Anyway, it wouldn't have lasted much longer; get this business in Calder over with and then for new pastures. He straightened his shoulders and quickened his pace.

He spent Friday counting noses and making guesses. Even the most optimistic of them gave Monk Malone an edge in the voting. A very slight edge, to be sure. One more good haul of Malone supporters and the balance might tip in favor of the Cleanup Party. And he did want the Cleanup Party to win. Not so much for the sake of Calder; he didn't give a hoot about the town's politics. But he wanted Molly to have the satisfaction of crowing over him and he did want the Rutherfords to enjoy their victory.

He visualized the face of Nancy when her faith in the right had been proved justified. That faith had been so unfaltering. He wondered a bit at the difference in his feelings toward the two girls. They were both lovely and wholesome young women, but there was a difference. He liked both of them immensely, but his liking for Nancy was more reserved, more reverent. Molly he liked as he would have liked a tomboy sister, only more—more— Aw, hell, why blind himself to the truth? If he loved her that was just his hard luck.

The outward quiet which had prevailed continued into Saturday. The FREE DRINKS FOR MINERS sign went up over the Frontier once more and by the time darkness fell the town was crowded. There was a lot of noise and there were a few fist fights, but no real disturbance. Bill arrested half a dozen of the fighters and lodged them in jail after Judge Higby had fined them. It was a mere gesture, but it made the judge happy and helped Bill keep up a front.

The shadower still kept on his trail, and Bill got quite a kick out of making his job as tough as he could.

Friday and Saturday had brought out new editions of the abbreviated *Clarion,* consisting of pep talks condensed into a paragraph or two. The feather duster had been entirely discarded and Bill had to concede that these articles must have some effect on the more timid citizens.

Sunday morning slid by dully, became an afternoon of gradually increasing tempo and ran into a night of heated argument and more fights. Bill became suddenly diligent, arresting miners and cowboys right and left. He appeared to be working hard for Malone but wasn't. Election day was drawing very near and men in jail couldn't get drunk or shot. The less hang-overs and deaths on Tuesday, the more cleanup votes. Probably as a sign of approval from Monk, the shadower was called off. His absence suited Bill's plans to a T. That night in the Double Eagle Bill slipped in beside Wes Peters and whispered, "Midnight. Same place."

At eleven o'clock he started his plan moving. It was an audacious plan, a dangerous one. He had selected six men who were wanted for crimes ranging from theft to murder. He moved about the various dives singling them out. He said to each, "Be at Cherokee's cabin at twelve. Go alone and be sure nobody sees you. Wait inside the shack. Some of the other boys'll join you there. Monk has something on tap but he doesn't want us to meet at the Frontier because the Cleanup bunch will be watching the place. And not a peep to anyone about this. Savvy?"

By eleven forty-five he had notified all six. He got his horse and rode to the Gospel tent and found Wes and his five boys waiting. He told them what he had planned.

"You boys will stay in a bunch and out of sight. I'll walk in on the six in the cabin and light a lamp. I'll go into a spiel about a raid on the gulch and hold their attention while you close in.

Be careful. It's risky, but we got to do it. I didn't tell them to fetch their horses, but Pete Stacy's down at the Frontier and there's nobody around the livery corral. A couple of you can hitch a team to a wagon and park it somewhere near the shack. We'll load them into that."

Wes said, "You're the feller that's takin' the risk, walkin' in on that bunch. If they smell a rat it'll be just too bad for you."

"We'll have to play them as they fall, Wes. If they smell a rat we'll hope they don't think it's me. This'll be our last roundup before election, and I couldn't think of any better way of getting six of them in a bunch. If things break bad, get out of here in a hurry. No silly ideas about getting me out. Ride to the county seat and tell the sheriff about it. Wes, take one of your boys and hitch up that team; the rest of you take positions under those trees behind Cherokee's shack. I'll wait five minutes before I go to the shack; that'll give you time to hitch up and park the wagon. When you see the light in the cabin, start closing in."

They left, Wes and another man riding toward the livery stable, the other four circling so as to reach the trees from the far side. Bill waited, mentally ticking off the minutes. He saw that his gun was fully loaded, even to the chamber beneath the hammer which he usually left empty. When he judged that the five minutes had expired, he started for the shack.

He tied his horse to a tree fifty yards from the cabin and went ahead on foot. He did not skulk and he did not hesitate. Half a dozen pairs of eyes would be watching his approach and he must walk boldly as though there was no deceit in him. The door was open but it was so dark inside that he couldn't see a thing. The silence almost shrieked.

He felt the hair at the back of his neck rise in warning; an uneasy feeling that all was not well gripped him, but he could not hesitate now. Although his nerves were keyed to the highest pitch and every muscle was ready to tauten, his voice as he stepped over the doorsill was casual.

"You fellers all here?"

"You're damned right we're here!" came the vicious reply. "Let the lousy double-crosser have it, boys!"

He strung it out just a second too long. Already warned by his hunch, the venom in the voice was all the confirmation Bill needed. Before the first sentence was fairly out Bill crouched and leaped to the left and into the blackness of a corner.

It was instinctive, the immediate response of a brain trained to reason swiftly in emergencies and the reaction of a body perfectly coordinated with that brain. The men would be bunched at the far end of the room where they would be safe from their own searching lead, and once out of the doorway Bill would not be visible to them.

A blast like thunder shook the shack and orange flame leaped from the muzzles of half a dozen Colts. The fire was concentrated on the open doorway and to both sides of it, and Bill heard the swish of lead through the air and the crash of its impact as slugs ripped through the walls.

He was flat on the floor and his gun was out but he did not fire, for the flash of his gun would only mark his position. He recalled the location of the furniture as he had seen it through the window the night they had taken Cherokee. Under cover of the shots which continued to pour from their guns he crawled along the wall to the end of a bunk. He went under it like a lizard, crawled to the upper end and lay quiet.

The firing ceased and a voice said, "You figger we got him?"

"How could we miss?" one of them wanted to know. "One of you take the lamp into a corner and light it."

Bill heard the sound of movement as an outlaw tried to locate the table, then the sounds approached the bunk and stopped in the corner. A match flamed within five feet of Bill's head and from beneath the bunk he saw the figure of a crouched man. The fellow had set the lamp on the floor and was gaining apprehensively toward the front of the cabin. Not seeing a six gun leveled at him, he raised the chimney of the lamp and applied flame to the wick.

From without the cabin came the sound of pounding feet, and one of the outlaws said, "A bunch of fellers comin' at the run!"

"What did you expect?" demanded the one who was evidently their leader. "The shootin' will fetch damned near the whole town. Bring that lamp out here where we can see."

The man with the lamp moved cautiously forward, holding the light at arm's length ahead of him. He had his Colt in his other hand and his eyes darted fearfully about. The whole six edged toward the doorway, following the creeping arc of yellow, crouched over, guns ready.

Bill slid out from under the bunk, came around on his knees and leveled his .44 over the head of the bed. A man said, "Hell! He ain't—!" and whirled. He saw Bill and his gun whipped into line. Bill shot him through the head.

He fired again as they wheeled, knocked another man down, snapped a shot at a third, then ducked behind the bunk as answering shots sent slugs tearing through it. He put his head and shoulders beneath the bunk and could see only the feet of them. He fired and another outlaw collapsed, his leg broken. They were shooting at the bunk now and keeping their shots low, and splinters flew as their lead ripped into the floor.

And then Wes's voice rang out. "Hold it! We got you covered!"

The firing ceased at once. Wes cried anxiously, "Bill, you all right?"

Bill crawled out from under the bunk. "All present and accounted for. Quick, boys! The whole town'll be here in a minute. Disarm these birds and get 'em out of here. Two of you carry the one with the broken leg; don't bother with the two on the floor, they're dead. Make it fast!"

They worked like beavers. The man who held the lamp stood with it in his hand. He had dropped his gun and was holding that hand as high in the air as he could push it. Bill took the lamp from him and put it in a corner where it would give them enough light to work by but would not reveal them so plainly to anyone outside.

Guns and knives were taken from the four living outlaws, their wrists were bound. The three sound prisoners were hustled from the room by three of the cowboys while the wounded man was carried by two others. Wes and Bill followed them into the darkness and ran for their horses.

Bill said, "Here are the wanted notices for all six. Take 'em to the county seat first thing in the morning. Get home before sundown on Tuesday if you have to kill some horses doing it. The Cleanup Party'll need your votes and I'll need your guns."

He left Wes and headed for the tree where his horse was tied. He mounted, rode a short distance away and sat waiting. He heard the rattle of wheels and saw the wagon heading for the ranch with the team at a gallop. From the direction of the main street came the sound of shouted questions and pounding boots. Running figures rounded the livery stable and headed for Cherokee's shack.

Bill circled to the street, tied his horse near the livery stable and ran after the bunch that were now crowding into Cherokee's cabin. He pushed through a few who had remained outside the doorway and halted on the threshold. Several men were on their knees by the dead outlaws, evidently making an examination; the others were poking about the room, guns in hands, seeking to discover what had happened.

Bill shouted, "Hold everything! What's going on in here? Who did this?"

Smoke Rafferty wheeled, but Bill had him under his gun and Smoke could not make his play just then. He grated, "That's what I'm askin' you."

"I just got here myself," Bill told him coldly. "What happened?"

Smoke made an angry gesture. "You can see, can't you? Two of the boys dead and no sign of the feller that did it. By grab, this thing has got to stop!"

Bill backed out and walked away. He had shown himself at the scene of the killings for Monk's benefit. Smoke was suspicious, but Bill's prompt appearance had left him puzzled. He moved away into the darkness grinning to himself. He was thinking of the six votes that had been lost to Malone this night.

CHAPTER THIRTEEN

MONK MALONE was furious. For the first time Bill was getting a good look at the man. Malone had risen from his desk and was stamping up and down the office as he raged. His gross, untidy body quivered with exertion and anger.

Standing near the side door was Smoke Rafferty, composed but alert, his mean eyes glinting. Bill stood near the opposite wall, equally composed, equally alert, equally glinting of eye. It looked very much as though the showdown had come and Bill was not ready for it yet.

"You can't deny you done it this time," raged Malone. "One of them fellers was suspicious and come to me before he went to the shack. I told him I never sent no message to meet at Cherokee's and he said that bein' the case he'd damned well take care of you. And I said for him to go ahead. You'd double-crossed me just one time too often."

"So you told him to go ahead and polish me off without even asking me what it was all about," said Bill tightly. "How come you didn't send your pet rattler to do the job?" He jerked his head toward Rafferty.

Monk halted and glared at him. "Smoke wasn't handy. He was around town somewheres but I didn't have time to find him. And I sure enough wasn't goin' to set and listen to a pack of your lies. I told him to go ahead and fix your clock for you."

Bill said, "I gave him that message, using your name, because it was the only way I could get him down to that shack where I could talk to him without being disturbed. I had an idea."

He was picking his words carefully. Two dead men had been found at Cherokee's; if one of them was the man who had gone to Monk, Malone would not know that there had been more in the deal than just those two. If the man who had seen him was one of the four prisoners, Monk would know that there were at least three in the party. Monk's next words set him right on this.

"I'll say you had an idea! You had the idea that you could get them two fellers down there and bump 'em both off. And you did."

Bill said, "Sit down, Monk, and listen to me. No use getting all stirred up. You got your own little graft, I thought I'd have one of my own. I knew both those hairpins are wanted outside for murder. One's Cole Brant and the other's Ed Foley. I was going to talk things over with them and come to some sort of understanding. After all I'm marshal of Calder; I could threaten to turn them in if they didn't come across."

Monk sat down behind the desk and regarded him with beady eyes. "How come you knew they was wanted?"

"I saw some notices that fitted them."

"Yeah? Where did you see them notices?"

"They come in every mail. The desk down at the jail is stuffed with them."

It sounded logical enough and Monk lost some of his belligerence. He frowned heavily, once more uncertain. Smoke noticed it and said harshly, "He's bluffin'. Don't let him make a sucker of you again, Monk."

"You keep out of this, lap dog!" grated Bill. "Monk's got brains; he can think for himself." He mentally crossed his fingers as he said it.

"Yeah," agreed Monk. "You stand hitched, Smoked." He turned back to Bill. "How come you killed 'em?"

Bill thought swiftly. He had tried to leave the impression that he had reached the scene after the two men were dead; he wanted that impression to remain. He said, "Kill them? Me? Smoke can tell you I didn't even get there until it was all over. I heard the shooting when I was on my way, but at that Smoke and some of the boys beat me there."

"That straight, Smoke?"

"He showed up after we got there, yes; but he could have been there before and come back."

Bill shrugged when Monk looked at him. "I could cook up a lie right easy and you'd never know the difference. Why don't you check with the feller you've had tailing me for the past week?"

"There wasn't nobody tailin' you."

"There sure was. I spotted him the other night but I had nothing to hide so I didn't bother about him. Of course, he might not have been one of your bunch; maybe the Cleanup gang's interested in where I go and what I do."

"Yeah," agreed Monk a little too readily. "Yeah, that must be it."

"All right, then; answer me this: Why should I shoot those two jaspers? I was figuring on shaking them down for a couple hundred apiece."

"That's easy," said Rafferty. "They wouldn't come across."

"I told you once to keep out of this. But since you found an answer to that one, find one for this: How did I manage to get both of them without collecting some lead myself? One, maybe; but two gunslingers who were already suspicious and watching for my play—! It just don't make sense, does it, Monk?"

"No," growled Monk, "it don't. I been wonderin' about that. The way Smoke put it I was sure you'd done it. I ain't sure yet that you didn't. If you hadn't been runnin' in Cleanup fellers right and left the last few days I'd take your badge and mebbe turn Smoke loose on you. Looked for a while there like you was workin' for the Cleanup outfit. It's got me buffaloed. Harrigan gets bumped off and I don't know nothin' about it; then Cherokee Smith and three pals disappear after a shootin' match; then four more of my best boys show up missin'; and now Brant and Foley are stiff and cold after another shootin'. What's happenin' to them? Where are they goin'?"

Bill said, "Fellers like them have grudges among themselves that nobody else knows about. They wouldn't mention it to you because you might put your foot down on their settling them. Most of 'em are killers; they wouldn't stop at ambushing each other if they really meant business."

That explanation didn't satisfy even the thick-headed Malone. He made a violent gesture and said, "Git out. Let me think it over."

Bill said, "Sure, Monk. You'll figure it out all right. You're smart."

He reached behind him and opened the door, then backed out and closed it. He smiled grimly. The show-down had been postponed, and the flattery had done it. He had seen Monk expand when he had called him smart. The best way to make an ignorant cluck swell up is to tell him he's smart.

The town was humming, but people gave him plenty of elbow room as he went up the street. He was acquiring a reputation as a gunman. Everybody knew of the disappearance of Cherokee and his pals, and now the word had gone around that he had single-handed worsted two of the best gunmen in Calder. Such feats of prowess entitled him to respect.

The *Clarion* office was lighted and he saw the five leaders of the Cleanup Party in conference. He went in. Molly turned her head and saw him and her face brightened. "Fred has just been telling us about it, Bill. Did you really shoot two of Malone's men?"

"I'd like to know how stories of that kind start," said Bill peevishly. "Monk Malone just got through accusing me of the same thing and I asked him how in the world I could out-shoot two of them at the same time without getting plugged. Not that I'd duck the chance of getting them if it came my way, for both of 'em were wanted for murder."

"How did you know that?" asked Sivart.

"Reward notices. In the jail desk."

"Well, whoever did it should get a vote of thanks. That's two votes Malone won't get."

Nancy's eyes were troubled. "It's two more murders. I'm afraid we won't enjoy a victory won at the expense of human lives."

"Doesn't the Bible say something about an eye for an eye and a tooth for a tooth?" asked Bill. "They got John Turner and Tom Harrigan and lose two killers in return. Not a fair exchange, but a good starter. But when you say Malone's lost two votes you're off your court. The latest returns show that Monk has lost fourteen votes in the past week."

"Fourteen!" cried Molly.

"That's right. These two dead ones and twelve who have just dropped out of sight during the week."

Sivart said, "Twelve? I thought it was eight."

Molly said, "Why, Fred! You never mentioned that some of Malone's men were missing."

"I didn't want to raise your hopes, Molly. The disappearance may only be temporary; they may come back for the election."

"Well, the total stands at fourteen, as far as I can figure it," said Bill. "I may be off one or two." He had made a slip, for he wasn't supposed to know about the four who had disappeared the night before. It was fortunate, he thought, that he was among friends.

"I'm glad to hear that the total has swelled," said Fred Sivart. "Perhaps Malone's bunch is beginning to see the handwriting on the wall. We're going to win the election tomorrow, Bill."

"Count noses right close, Fred, and if you find you're shy some votes let me know and I'll bump off a few more." He caught the startled look on Nancy's face and said quickly, "Forgive me, Nancy. I was only fooling."

"It isn't right even to joke about such things," she reproved. "You should remember that he who lives by the sword shall perish by the sword."

"Nancy, I wish I could agree with you all the time, but I just can't. I reckon I was weaned on a six gun. And of all the Bible stories my mother used to tell me when I was a kid I somehow always remember the ones where the Lord sent forth men to fight for Him. Like David. Only difference between David and me is that he used stones and I used bullets."

Rutherford chuckled and said, "I guess he got you there, daughter." But Nancy simply smiled at Bill and shook her golden head. Bill told them good night and left.

That Monday was a hectic day, both sides making their last-minute efforts to convince voters. In Malone's case the word was intimidate rather than convince; he was sure of his votes, he strove to fix it so that the Cleanup Party could not be sure of theirs. The free-drinks sign remained above the Frontier entrance and miners declared a holiday to take full advantage of it. They were drunk all over the place.

The Malone forces held a torchlight parade that night. They were out in full regalia, including six guns and rifles. It was very imposing. They were strung out in two long files and Bill suspected that some of them ducked into alleys and circled the block in order to pass in review a second time. At three o'clock in the morning the Frontier closed and drunken miners weaved their ways to the gulch or were helped there by roughs. Bill had never seen Malone's hard-bitten criminals so gentle and tenderhearted. He suspected a purpose in their kindness but could not sense what it was.

He went to the polling place in Hollister's store bright and early on Tuesday morning. The election board had already assembled. For Malone there were a rough named Martin, Joe Haynes of the Gold Standard and Blackie White, another saloonkeeper. For the Cleanup Party there were Leander and Molly Sexton and Reverend Rutherford. Molly handed Bill a printed sheet from a stack on the counter, and he read:

The Cleanup Party's Candidate for Mayor
ALFRED SIVART
Councilmen
Henry Hollister—Benjamin Shotten—Howard Wilson

So Fred Sivart was the mystery candidate. Bill had hoped that Leander Sexton, having lost the *Clarion,* would decide to run. Hollister was the owner of the store; Shotten and Wilson were both miners. Putting their names on the ballot was, he supposed, an inducement for the miners to come out and vote.

A number of Malone's roughs hung about outside the store with the evident purpose of intimidating voters. Bill took his stand where he could watch them, determined to toss them into the jug if they stepped out of line. Tradesmen went into the store, cast their votes and came out again looking apprehensive or defiant according to their natures. There were a number of grim-faced women about the store, probably to make sure that the courage of their menfolk did not dissolve under the glares of the Malone roughs.

Bill left his post occasionally to prowl about town, keeping his eyes and ears open. He checked on Frank Cade at the Double Eagle, then found the cabin where the man lived, discovered that the door was unlocked and went in. He searched the place thoroughly, but found nothing to indicate that Frank was the power behind the throne occupied by Monk Malone.

He missed Smoke Rafferty and a bartender at the Frontier told him that the gunman was not in Malone's office. He didn't see Smoke all morning and the fellow's absence worried him. An uneasy hunch that something was in the wind gripped him and made him restless and apprehensive. Those hunches had proven correct so many times that he had learned to respect them.

The town began to fill up after dinner. Cowboys from outlying ranches rode in, voted, then went to the Double Eagle to await the result of the election. Wes and his five would not be in until late in the afternoon. Monk's roughs drifted in and voted one or two at a time, stringing it out, and the Cleanup Party's board members kept a sharp eye on them to prevent duplication. Not one of the miners had come up from the gulch yet. Shortly after noon Monk Malone waddled into the store and voted. Smoke Rafferty was with him and Bill felt better. It was the first time since Bill had arrived in Calder that Monk had appeared on the street.

Bill cast his own vote around three in the afternoon, and when he came out of the booth Molly stopped him. "I'm getting worried about the miners. It's getting late and we simply must have their votes to win. And Wes and his boys haven't come in yet. What can be keeping them?"

"You can count on Wes," he told her. "They may not get here until the last minute, but they'll be here. I don't know about the miners, but they're probably suffering from hangovers. Monk didn't leave that free-drinks sign up just because he's kind-hearted. They'll probably come in a bunch just before the polls close at sundown."

"They better had, or we're sunk. Bill, why don't you ride down to the gulch and get them started?"

He was beginning to become worried himself; he said he would and got his horse and rode down. The long toms along the creek were idle and there wasn't a soul in sight. Bill went into the first shack he came to and heard heavy snores before he had crossed the threshold. He found the miner sprawled across his bunk, arms dangling, feet spread, snoring his life away.

Bill shook him and slapped him and got no response other than some thickly muttered words. He bent over and got a good whiff of the man's breath. It was laden with whiskey and something else. Bill sniffed at the tin cup which had fallen from the man's hand to the floor. What was that alien odor? Was it laudanum?"

He hurried to another shack and found the same conditions there. He also found it in the next, and the next, and the next.

Miners were sprawled in bunks, in chairs, on the floor. All of them slept the sleep of the dead; every one of them had been drugged.

And now Bill could make a good guess where Smoke Rafferty had been that morning. He had taken a liberal supply of doped whiskey to the gulch and had poured it into gullets of miners still so drunk that they didn't know what they were drinking. He knew also why these miners had been so tenderly helped to their shacks in the gulch. Down here the day would be almost gone before they were discovered, and then it would be too late. And the loss of the miner's vote meant the loss of the election to Molly and Nancy and their followers.

He rode back to the store as rapidly as horseflesh could carry him.

"Looks like the Cleanup Party's sunk," he reported grimly to Molly. "Every miner in the gulch has been doped with doctored whiskey. They won't come out of it before night and then they won't care who's elected."

The despair which came into her face made him wince. "But we've got to have their votes! We just must! Somehow we've got to get them up here. Bill, you can do it! You're the only man who can!"

"I doubt if there's any man who can do it. But I know a woman who might. Where's Nancy?"

"At the Gospel tent, I suppose. Bill, what can she do?"

"She's an angel, ain't she? Well, we sure need help from heaven to put this election over." He turned to Hollister. "Grind up five pounds of coffee: I'll stop for it on my way back."

Molly followed him to the door, anxiously asking what he intended to do, but he waved back and vaulted into his saddle. He rode up to the tent and told the story quickly to Nancy. "We've got to go down and pour black coffee into them. We've got to get them on their feet and moving around. I can't do it alone. They worship you and you can do a lot with them. You have a horse and wagon; I'll hitch up and put the melodeon in it. We'll need it."

They stopped at the store long enough to get the coffee, then went on to the gulch, Nancy driving, Bill riding beside her. They built a fire in a stove and collected half a dozen coffeepots from as many shacks. They brewed coffee strong enough to walk, then went to work.

The miners were as sluggish as sloths. Nancy and Bill poured coffee into them, almost scalding them out of their stupor. One by one Bill got them on their feet and walking, Nancy on one side, Bill on the other. It seemed useless; when they left one to tackle another, the first one promptly flopped to the floor and went to sleep again.

Bill said, "Get out to that wagon and start playing like hell!"

She went out and struck up *Suzanna*. Bill hauled a miner from his bunk and said, "Come on, partner, let's dance!" He pushed and pulled the doped man about the floor until at last the fellow began moving his feet. It was quite a trick to get two of them together, but once he succeeded the two kept shuffling automatically, and Bill thanked his stars that the miners were, as Biff had put it, suckers for dancing.

He ran to another shack, calling to Nancy to keep playing, and started a wrestling match with another pair. Within another hour feet were shuffling in a dozen shacks and Nancy was squeezing *Suzanna* out of the little organ for the sixtieth time.

After that it came easier. More coffee and plenty of profanity. Bill did not spare Nancy's feelings, but spoke to them in the language they understood. Nancy started singing. Bill herded the dancing pairs out into the open air and turned loose a violent tirade. "Listen to her! Singing her heart out for a bunch of worthless bums! Are you going to let her down? Going to let Malone make suckers of you? Come on, get your feet to tracking! Come to Calder and vote!"

They went. They followed the wagon in a stumbling, weaving procession, their very efforts sweating alcohol and drug from their bodies. Bill brought up in the rear like a drag rider behind a herd of cattle, urging, prodding, cursing. The sun was touching the horizon when they staggered into the end of the street and straightened out for the store.

Bill heard a wild chorus of yips and looked over the herd to see Wes and his cowboys come rushing along the street to help. They fell in on both sides of the column, ready and anxious to give them protection from the roughs if they needed it. They stumbled up the steps of the store and into the booths and voted.

Outside a revolver barked to announce that the polls were closed. The election board started to count the votes. Bill, standing in the doorway to keep out the crowd, heard Molly's exultant cry and turned to see Leander Sexton mounting a stepladder with a roll of canvas under his arm. He tacked a corner to the wall and started unrolling it, tacking as he went. The word WINS! was revealed. The last letter of the winner's name came into view, then the next to the last and so on until the two words stood revealed. The banner read: SIVART WINS.

A small cyclone hit Bill. Arms went about his neck and hugged him and a pair of lips smacked fervently against his cheek. Molly cried, "Bill, we did it! We did it! *We won by six votes!*"

Bill heard her as in a dream. He was almost unconscious of the kiss. He had watched the banner unfold, and as he watched the veil was lifted and he saw and understood and was dumb with astonishment and comprehension. He stared over Molly's dark head at the banner. He read it again as he had read it when it was unrolled. It was true; it wasn't just coincidence.

He was aware of Nancy standing at his side. Her face was smiling and the blue eyes were very bright. Never before had she appeared so like an angel. She spoke to Bill, "I told you the right would prevail. Bill, you must never doubt again."

CHAPTER FOURTEEN

MOLLY WAS SHAKING HIM. "Bill! You're like a post! Don't you understand? *We won!*"

He blinked and shook the cobwebs from his brain and looked down at her. "Did we?"

"Of course. Can't you read? At any rate, I won. And you owe me a lifetime of service—dishwashing, bed-making, type cleaning. Bill, for goodness' sake wake up!"

Bill looked over her shoulder and into the face of Fred Sivart. He said, "Well, you made it. Pretty close, wasn't it?"

Fred was smiling with his lips. He had seen that kiss and he hadn't liked it. "You don't seem very enthusiastic. But you swung it for me, Bill; you and Nancy. I'm sure I speak for the new council when I say that we want you to remain as marshal."

"Thanks. I'll stick around until things settle down." He looked again at Molly and animation returned to him. "You girls better find a place where you'll be safe. There's no telling how Malone's crowd is going to take this."

Her chin went up. "We're not afraid of them, are we, Nancy? We beat them at the polls, we can beat them at anything they start."

"Don't talk foolish," he told her impatiently. "The miners will be no good to us if it comes to a fight. Fred, take them out to the Turner ranch, will you? It's the safest place I can think of."

"Good idea, Bill; I'll do it."

"But I don't want to go," protested Molly.

He gripped her by the shoulders and shook her until the dark curls bobbed. He spoke roughly, almost savagely. "Listen to me, you stubborn little brat! You climb into the buggy with Fred and get yourself out to that ranch where I won't have to worry about you."

Her eyes went wide and her jaw sagged. For an instant she returned his fierce glare with one that matched it; then slowly the fire went out of her eyes and the black-fringed lashes dropped. She said meekly, "Yes, Bill."

He left the girls with Fred and went out through the doorway. Malone's roughs had gone; he could see some of them running toward the Frontier with the news of Malone's defeat. Wes and his cowboys were there and Bill said, "I'm deputizing all of you. Let's go up to the Double Eagle and gather all the hands we can. I've a hunch we're going to need them."

They rode up the street and on the way to the Double Eagle Wes made his report. The prisoners had been delivered, after which he and the boys had got a few hours' sleep and then had started back immediately.

"Sheriff give you any message for me?"

"Yes. Said what you expected hadn't come through yet but should arrive any minute—whatever it is."

"You'll find out later, I hope. Right now we got a job of work on our hands. Wes, I've just tumbled to the whole setup and I'm still in a fog. The thing is so downright clever that I'm dizzy. I don't know how these roughs are going to react. It'll be one of two ways: either they'll sit tight and do nothing, or they'll start taking the town apart. If I got it figured out right it'll be the latter."

Wes said, "Fine! That'll give us the chance we've been waitin' for ever since John was shot. We'll shoot our way through the Frontier, drag Monk Malone down to the livery corral and string him up over the gate."

"Take it from me, that would be a mistake. Monk didn't give the order to kill Turner or flash the signal to Sam Sneed. All the time Monk has been merely a front for somebody else."

Wes was shaken. "Good grief, Bill, who? You certainly owe it to us to tell us. Who?"

Bill considered for a moment. "Not just yet, Wes. I want to get the proof first. I think I'll find it at the Double Eagle, and when there's no doubt about it, I'll tell you."

"And when you get it," asked Wes tightly, "can I count on your lettin' us handle him?"

"You can. The law would doubtless execute him, but you boys are entitled to the job and you'll have it. Right now do one thing for me: keep your eye on Frank Cade every minute."

"Is he the man?"

"I'm quite sure he's mixed up in it somewhere. Just watch him. If he tries to get in touch with Monk, stop him. No violence; just hold him."

They dismounted before the Double Eagle and stood for a moment listening to the sounds which rolled across the street from the Frontier. They were sinister sounds, the babble of excited voices, the shuffling of restless feet, angry oaths and an occasional shout. There was no longer any doubt in Bill's mind; the roughs weren't going to sit tight. Realizing that they had lost their protection, they were bent on wrecking the town before they scattered in the hills.

"We'd better hurry," said Bill. "And it would be a good idea to get the horses off the street."

They led the animals to a place behind the alley and left them there. They entered the Double Eagle by the rear door.

The place was crowded with celebrating cowboys and trades-people and a few hardy miners. They were flushed with victory and were buying drinks as fast as the bartenders could serve them. Frank Cade sat at the faro table, stony of face, idly shuffling a deck of cards. Bill thrust through the crowd, elbowed a man away from the bar and leaped to its surface. His violence and the grimness of his face caught their attention and they became quiet.

He said, "No more drinks will be sold. Malone's men are going on the warpath and we'll need every man, every gun, if we expect to stop them. The miners are out on their feet; they'll be of little use to us. You cowboys, get your horses off the street. Anybody who isn't packing a gun, come with me to the jail and I'll distribute what weapons we have there. I'm not fooling; within the next half hour Calder's going to live up to its reputation of being the Devil's Doorstep and Hell's Back Yard."

It sobered them like a dash of icy water and in the silence which followed they all heard the surge of angry sound from the Frontier and knew Bill was speaking the truth. The cowboys left their drinks and went for their horses; Bill jumped from the bar and started for the door, a dozen men at his heels. They followed him across the street to the jail, and as they passed the Lucky Tiger another wave of sound told them that outlaws were assembling here, too. Bill unlocked the door and went in and started passing out weapons from the rack and ammunition from the desk.

And then there reached them a sudden outbreak of increased sound, the wild yells of killers on the loose, the sudden thunder of six guns and the sharper cracks of rifles. In answer to it came yells of defiance and a scattered volley of gunfire.

Bill ran to the jail doorway. Up the street outlaws were pouring from the doors of the Frontier and across the street in the direction of the Double Eagle. They fired as they ran and answering shots blazed from the door and windows of Sivart's place, the orange streaks stabbing the dusk. Bill saw some of the outlaws stumble and fall before the mob split to right and left in search of cover.

He was about to call to his men to follow him when another mob burst from the Lucky Tiger next door. They wheeled to the right in the direction of the Frontier, but one of them, glancing over his shoulder, saw Bill and let out a yell of warning. It was the last sound he made. Bill shot him dead, kept thumbing the hammer of his .44. Two more men went down; then the mob had turned in its tracks and Bill leaped inside and slammed the heavy door as a gust of lead swept the place where he had been standing. He yelled, "Bar that back door—quick!" Several of his men ran into the corridor to obey the command.

The building was of adobe and as strong as a fort; there were two small front windows instead of a single big one. The panes of these went at once, blasted away by the mob; but the windows were set high in the wall and nobody inside the place was hit.

Bill said, "You four with the riot guns, get up to those windows and start throwing buckshot. Some of you others man the windows in the cells."

The door shook as heavy shoulders struck it, but it was solid and did not give. Lead continued to sweep through the front windows and flatten on the adobe walls. In the rear, other shoulders butted vainly against the back door. Four of the men, crouching low, moved to the front windows. Still keeping below the sills, they shoved their sawed-off shotguns through the openings and let fly. There were howls of rage and pain and gunfire abruptly ceased. From the direction of the Frontier came the sounds of furious fighting.

Bill went back into the corridor. Men were standing on bunks at the small barred windows of the cells, six-guns ready. They were unable to see or do anything but wait, but it would go hard with any outlaw who raised his head above the sills to take a pot shot at those inside. Two men stood with leveled rifles a few feet from the back door. Bill decided that the jail could hold out indefinitely, but got little satisfaction from the knowledge. The men in the Frontier needed help, and as things stood a large part of his force was being held immobile here by a smaller number of outlaws. And Bill, a man of action, felt that he was needed at the Frontier.

Dusk was rapidly changing to darkness. Bill went back into the office and called two of the men with riot guns to him and led them to the rear door. He said, "I'm going out; I've got to see how things are down the street. You boys with the scatter-guns cover me while I make a dash for the stable. You with the rifles, take down the bar and unlock the door. In the rear cells there! How do things look in the alley?"

A man peered through one of the small windows which overlooked the alley and answered, "Five or six of 'em out back. One behind a barrel, two behind a wagon at the right of the stable, two more inside, and I think there's one up in the hayloft."

"Boys, you heard him. You men with the riot guns, put a barrel each into the stable entrance, then hold your fire until something shows. You men at the windows, watch the barrel and the wagon. One of you riflemen cover the door in the loft. Got it? Okay; now open up and let the riot guns do their stuff."

He crouched beside the door. It was yanked open suddenly and the two with the riot guns stepped up and fired their buckshot through the stable doorway. Pushing in front of them, Bill took off like a sprinter doing a hundred-yard dash.

He made five of the ten yards between him and the doorway in a straight plunge, then started leaping zig-zag fashion. A gun flashed from the blackness within the stable and he fired at the spurt of flame and heard a grunt of agony. Then he was in the doorway. The man at whom he had fired was to his right; the other would probably be to the left. He turned in that direction, still running, and crashed solidly into a yielding body. He went down on top of the other and felt the burn of powder on his neck as the man's gun exploded. He struck savagely with the barrel of his .44 again and again. The last blow landed squarely and he felt and heard the squashy crack that told of a fractured skull.

He rolled clear and got to his feet, whirling to face the door. He saw one of his men raise the scatter-gun and let fly at the upstairs, then wheeled as a man came scampering down the ladder which led to the loft. He was just an indistinct shadow and his back was turned to Bill, but Bill shot him without any compunction whatever. The man tumbled from the ladder and lay in a heap at its foot.

Bill went on through the barn and came to the open ground in back of it. He stumbled along in the darkness, managing to punch out the empties and reload as he ran. He filled the cylinder completely, for he would need every bullet he could cram into the gun.

He thought fleetingly of Molly and Nancy and hoped they had got clear of the town before the outbreak. What was it he had told Molly? There would be looting and shooting and mud and blood. Well, his prediction was coming true. Certainly there was looting and shooting in Calder today, and certainly blood had been spilled. He had spilled his share. He would spill more before the day was done.

CHAPTER FIFTEEN

B ILL PASSED behind the Lucky Tiger and cut into the alley
where the going was better. He continued along the alley
toward the Frontier and suddenly smelled smoke. It was too dark
to see where it originated but he felt sure it was somewhere ahead
of him. His face tightened. Arson was being added to theft and
murder.

He reached the Frontier, opened the rear door and went inside.
There were no lights and the place was as gloomy as a graveyard.
Up in the front of the building some outlaws crouched below the
windows and were firing spasmodically at the Double Eagle across
the way. There was nobody in the back. Bill crossed to the office,
twisted the doorknob and went in, his gun extended before him.

He stepped to one side of the doorway and stood crouched
with the wall behind him, peering about in the darkness. So used
was he to finding Monk behind the desk that he half expected
to find him there now; but he saw nothing, heard no sound. He
glided in an arc to the front of the desk and saw against the lighter
blackness of the window behind it that Monk was not there. He
went around, sat down in the chair, struck a match with his left
hand and held the flame high so that it would not blind him. The
office was empty.

He lighted the lamp and turned the wick low, then went
through the desk swiftly and expertly. He found not a thing that
would aid in convicting Monk. He hadn't really expected to.
Malone's desk would be the first thing to be examined by members of the Cleanup Party and Monk knew it.

He blew out the light, went through the side door and into the passageway so often used by Smoke Rafferty. He moved up to the front and, crouching at the corner, looked across the street. Flashes came from the Double Eagle downstairs and up, but they were not so numerous or continuous as he would have liked them to be. Either the defenders had scattered and were holding their fire or they had suffered losses at the hands of Malone's roughs.

There was no chance of getting across to the Gold Standard here except by a quick dash, and that would be suicide. In the darkness he would not be recognized by the defenders and if he called out his identity he would he picked off by the riflemen in the Frontier. He went down the street a short distance and found a place where he could cross the street, and once on the other side he cut back to the alley and followed it. He met nobody until he came to the building beside the Gold Standard. Men were here, hiding behind stacks of boxes and inside sheds, keeping watch and pinning the defenders of the Gold Standard down. It looked like a stalemate and Bill breathed easier.

He went back down the alley, passing vague figures who paid him no attention, thinking him one of their number, and suddenly he saw a bright glow in the sky and made his way by the first passageway to the street. A burst of flame on the far side greeted him.

It was Hollister's store which was burning, and there was a mob of crazy, dancing figures in the street before it. More figures were running in and out of the building and those who came out were loaded down with merchandise. The whole rear of the store was a mass of flame. The front of the building cast a shadow over the street and the men there were distinguishable as shapes but not as definite individuals.

As Bill approached he saw a torch break into flame. The man who held it ran up the steps of the store and by its light Bill recognized Smoke Rafferty. Forgetting personal danger, Bill thrust his way through the shouting outlaws. In their excitement they seemed not to recognize him.

He went up the steps at a run and nearly stumbled over a sprawled body at their top. He stooped and rolled the man over. It was Hank Hollister and he had been shot through the head. Bill leaped over the body and went into the store.

Bolts of cloth and various articles taken from the counters had been piled in the middle of the floor and the reek of kerosene was in the air. Rafferty hurled the burning torch into its midst and it went up with a great *woosh!*

Smoke Rafferty turned to turn for the door and in the blaze recognized Bill. He seemed to freeze in mid-stride, a black silhouette against the flames. He was caught flat-footed, for Bill's gun was leveled at him and his own Colt was still in its holster. His hands went into the air and he cried, "Don't shoot! I give up!"

So the man was yellow after all. Bill's lip curled as he snarled, "No, you don't. You shoot, you stinking little snake!" He slid the gun into its holster and raised his hands to the same level as Rafferty's.

The man's back was to the flames and Bill could not see the expression on his face, but he knew what it was. It would reflect despair turned suddenly to jubilation, resignation into gloating. The fool marshal was going to play the game his way and he could not lose. Smoke's hands swept down with the speed of long and diligent practice.

Bill's hands moved every bit as fast. The right one fell unerringly on the walnut butt of the .44, then moved back and sharply down in a jerk that tilted the holster upward on its swivel. The Colt roared through the open bottom a quarter of a second before Smoke could fire. Rafferty's bullet gouged splinters from the floor at Bill's feet. Bill's lead struck Smoke squarely between the eyes.

Rafferty staggered backwards, his arms outflung and moving as though he were trying to recover his balance; but the slug had gone through his brain and he was already dead. He fell into the flaming pile and Bill walked forward as close as he could. He said, "Burn, you rotten little killer! I couldn't dream of a better end for you."

Slugs started whistling through the front doorway and Bill knew the outlaws in the street had recognized him and would not permit him to leave by the front entrance. The back of the store was blazing fiercely and he knew he could not make his way through the rear door alive. He ran to a side window and smashed out what remained of sash and pane with his gun. He wormed through the opening and dropped to the ground only to find himself in as hopeless a position as he had been inside the store. Flames had burst through the wall at the rear and closed that exit to him; the street in front was filled with outlaws.

The outlaws has seen Bill leave by the window and now they concentrated their fire on the passageway. Among them were friends of Biff Bang, of Cherokee Smith, of Smoke Rafferty; and now that the marshal had openly taken sides against them there remained no doubt in their minds. Bullets swept in a hail along the passageway and Bill dropped flat on the ground where he would not be revealed so clearly against the background of flame. He crowded against a wall and waited, withholding his fire lest the flash of the shot mark his position. One of the outlaws, bolder or more reckless than the rest, ventured into the passageway. He came in at the crouch, his gun extended. Bill fired then and shot him dead.

Swiftly he rolled across the lane and against the wall on the other side. Lead screeched over his body and thudded into the dirt beside him. He thought, *They'll get me here sure. Only a matter of time. I'd rather be on my feet when it comes.*

He got up, hugging the wall. He had four cartridges left in his gun and there would be no time to reload. He must make every one of them count. He leaped forward, firing.

And then above the noise and confusion he heard the pound of hoofs and the sudden roar of guns, and the forms of the outlaws in the street began to melt away. They were no longer facing in his direction but had turned to look up the street. He saw some of them raise their guns and fire, saw others fall in the dust; then the survivors had turned and were running wildly to escape the approaching menace.

Bill knew what that menace was. The Rangers he had been expecting had finally arrived.

He stopped at the front corner of the store and reloaded his gun, then walked out into the street, raising his right hand high. The horsemen had deployed in a line which extended from sidewalk to sidewalk, and they advanced at a steady walk, pressing forward as remorselessly as a juggernaut. Bill called, "Pull up there, Lieutenant!"

The line halted and the lieutenant said, "That you, Cap? Looks like you're havin' some fun for yourself."

"Where the hell you been? You were supposed to be here not later than sundown."

"This is the damndest country, Bill. We got on the wrong road and went twenty miles out of the way. But we knew you were on the job and didn't worry none. We figgered you could hold the fort for another hour or two."

"Yeah," said Bill sarcastically. "Too bad you got here so soon. I was just about to polish the rest of 'em off. Give me one of your stirrups and I'll mount up behind you. Ride straight along the street and shoot everything that doesn't throw away his hardware and push his hands in the air. Ride on, my brave lad, I'm right behind you."

The lieutenant turned his head to grin. "So I notice. That's what worries me."

CHAPTER SIXTEEN

THE TURNER ranch house was a scene of uneasy quiet. The only occupants who were not uneasy were the children, and they were in bed.

Inside the house, Mrs. Turner went about silently, straightening furniture that needed no straightening, opening and closing closets, peering often through the open doorway toward the rosy sky which told of flames in Calder. In a chair by the table, Reverend Rutherford read his Bible, but it was difficult for him to concentrate and he found his gaze drawn often to the ruddy glow.

Out on the gallery Molly Sexton and Nancy Rutherford sat in straightbacked, uncomfortable chairs, uneasy and fearful. Leander Sexton rocked back and forth nervously. Fred Sivart paced up and down, tense, anxious, his glance rarely leaving the reflection in the distant sky.

"It's awful, awful," said Nancy in a stricken voice. "And we thought all the fighting, all the trouble was over. Oh, why do men do such wicked things!"

"So that men like Bill can undo them," said Molly tightly. "And get killed doing it." Her voice had a note of hysteria in it.

Nancy said in a low voice, "You love Bill, don't you, Molly?"

"He saw my ring; he thinks I'm engaged."

"But you do love him, don't you?"

"Yes, Nancy, I do. I didn't realize it until now—now when he's over there fighting, killing, maybe being killed." The thought chilled her into a short silence; then she said, "You love him too, don't you?"

"No. I like him very much. In many ways he reminds me of another Bill I once knew. He was big and curly-headed and laughing, but they—they shot him. There can never be another one for me."

So at last Molly knew why this sweet, attractive girl never seemed drawn to any man. She said, "Nancy, I'm terribly sorry." She leaned over impulsively and put her arms about the slight, blonde girl.

Nancy said, "Bill loves you, Molly."

"Nancy!"

"He does. I know it."

Fred Sivart had turned; now he came over to stand looking down at the two girls. He said to Molly, "What was that you said about Bill? That you loved him?"

"Yes. I think I've loved him since the first time I saw him. I don't know why. He torments me and makes me mad and he's always so darned right! But I love him and I think I made it plain to him."

"I saw you throw your arms about him and kiss him there in the store," said Sivart tightly. "He acted as though he didn't know what you'd done. Or was it the kiss that put that dazed look on his face?" His voice was harsh, and for some reason it irked Molly.

She said, "I hope it was the kiss. If it wasn't, I'll keep on trying until it does."

"And I thought all along you cared a little for me," said Fred bitterly. "If you're so set on getting your man you ought to join the Rangers."

Nancy said matter-of-factly, "I believe Bill's a Ranger. One in the family should be enough."

Molly gasped and her father said, "What's that?"

Sivart snapped, "Bill a Ranger! What gave you that idea?"

"Lots of things. He's efficient, closemouthed, calm, sure of himself. And what brought him to Calder in the first place? He's well educated and neat and mannerly. He's no idle drifter and he most certainly isn't a fugitive from justice."

Sexton said, "But I wrote to the Rangers appealing for help, and your father wrote to the Governor himself. All we got in reply was the vague promise of help some time in the future."

Molly was putting a few little things together, and her eyes brightened with the conviction that Nancy was right. "What did you expect, Dad—a definite promise that a company of Rangers would arrive in Calder at ten A.M. on October 25th? You'd print it in the *Clarion* and Malone's whole flock would be tipped off. I'm quite sure Nancy's right."

"Somebody's coming," said Sivart in a sharp voice. He was leaning over the edge of the gallery, his head cocked like that of a bird dog.

"It may be Malone's roughs," said Sexton. "We'd better go inside."

A distant shout came ringing over the range. *Yip! Yip! Yip-e-e-e!*

"That's Wes and the boys," said Mrs. Turner from the doorway. "They always let out that yell when they sight the house."

"We'll know the worst now," said Sexton in a tight voice. "The miners couldn't help and Malone's men are so well organized."

Rutherford had followed Mrs. Turner to the door. He said in a ringing voice, "That was not a cry of defeat! That was a shout of victory! I know it! I feel it! Friends, the Lord has listened to our prayers."

A group of horsemen came sweeping over the starlit rangeland and pulled up before the house. A tall man swung from his horse and came striding up the steps and Molly cried "Bill!" and flung herself at him. And this time he wasn't too dazed to realize that he held a hundred and ten pounds of desirability in his arms and her fervent kiss did not go unanswered.

There was another man with Wes and his cowboys. He was black-haired and black-coated and once he had been suave. Right now he bestrode a horse with his hands bound to the saddle horn and he looked rather the worse for wear. One of the men untied him and dragged him from his horse and he was brought up on the veranda.

Sivart said, "Cade! What are they doing to you?"

"I don't know," said Cade. "They're just crazy.'"

Bill kissed Molly again and then turned to them. "Let's go into the house and I'll explain what we're doing to Cade." He led the way, his arm still about Molly.

When they were all in the big living room, Wes said with a wide grin, "Folks, meet up with Captain Bill Borden of the Rangers. He sure had us all fooled to a fare-you-well. But Rangers don't talk until the job is finished. The Governor sent him in answer to Reverend Rutherford's letter to sort of look over the ground and get things lined up so that his boys could come in and gather the flock into the fold without wastin' any time. And I'll tell a man they did some gatherin' tonight."

"Tell us about it," urged Sexton. "We saw the fire and we've been on edge waiting for news."

So Wes told them of the battle in Calder and of its dramatic climax. The store was gone, so was Hank Hollister and another of the newly elected councilmen. Several cowboys from other ranches had been killed and a number of them wounded, but except for minor wounds all the Turner crew had escaped injury. More than a dozen outlaws had been killed, twice that many wounded, and the jail and the livery corral held the rest, with Rangers to guard them.

"What about Malone and Smoke Rafferty?" asked Sexton.

"Smoke stopped lead somewhere along the line," Bill told them. "We gathered in Malone. Found him hiding under a bed. Might have missed him at that but he's so fat that the bed bulged."

"He must be tried and hanged for his crimes," said Sexton. "He was the cause of all the evil and bloodshed."

"No," contradicted Bill, "he wasn't. Very soon after I met him I decided that he was only a front for somebody else. Monk was stupid, ignorant; the man behind this show was smart and educated and infinitely more dangerous than Malone could ever be."

Sexton was frowning. "Bill, are you sure? All the evidence we have points straight to Malone as the source of evil in this town."

"The visible source, Mr. Sexton; but all the time he was acting under orders from somebody else. Just before this protection racket started a suave stranger moved into Calder. He was an outlaw named Al Travis and he was wanted for murder a couple times over. He wanted to assemble about him a large number of equally desperate men, a force large enough to protect themselves—and him—from any posse which might venture into Calder. So he let it be known that he would give protection to wanted men for a price and worked his scheme through Malone, who was mayor and who received a commission for his services."

They all looked at Frank Cade. Sexton said, "So it was Cade all the time! Oh, it's very simple now, isn't it? He worked for Fred and learned things, secrets of the Cleanup Party. He was a councilman and used his position to keep in touch with Malone. Yes, it's very plain now."

"No, it isn't," said Bill. He took a circular from his pocket and opened it. "This is a wanted notice bearing Travis's description. It fits Frank Cade rather well except for three things. Travis had light hair. Frank's hair is black, but hair can be dyed so we might say it fits him except for two things. Travis has blue eyes, and Cade's are black. A man can't change the color of his eyes. Travis has a six-inch knife scar on his chest—*Grab him, boys!*"

Fred Sivart had started backing toward the door, his glinting eyes fixed on Bill and his hand on the butt of his Colt. When Bill mentioned the knife scar he turned and leaped; and he leaped right into the arms of two of the cowboys who had quietly placed themselves between the group and the door. He struggled fiercely, but the other boys sprang to the aid of their companions and he was held quiet while Wes wrenched the gun from its holster.

Sivart grated, "Let me go! The man's crazy!"

"Not quite as crazy as you wish I was," Bill told him grimly. He came forward and, gripping Sivart's shirt, gave a sudden jerk. There was a rip and the front of a silk undershirt was exposed. Sivart strained and tried to break away; he lashed out with his foot, but Bill side-stepped and seized the neck of the undershirt and yanked again. The cloth tore and the buttons flew and there on his chest was a livid scar just about six inches long.

Bill said, "When I realized that Malone was fronting for somebody my suspicions were directed to Cade because of the reasons given by Mr. Sexton. I hadn't checked on the color of his eyes or the scar, but I didn't need to. The whole thing was made clear when Mr. Sexton unrolled the strip of canvas with the words SIVART WINS! painted on it. For he unrolled it from right to left; I saw the word WINS! first, and then, letter by letter, came the name of the winner, but with the letters reversed. And read that way the words spelled T-R-A-V-I-S.

"From the first time I looked at that notice I had the feeling that I knew that name. I must have glanced back at the name and subconsciously read it in reverse. And notice how the Al fits. When he rode the owlhoot trail he was Al Travis; as a respected citizen of Calder he became Alfred Sivart. All right, boys. I hate to wish the trip on you, but you'd better take him to town and turn him over to the Rangers. Lock Cade in the stable before you go; I want to question him later. He was the go-between, of course, and I think he'll come clean now that his protection is gone."

They hustled the two men from the room, and Cade was securely locked in the strong stable. They put Travis on a horse and roped him there and then slipped the noose of a lariat about his neck just to make sure. They rode toward town and when they had put distance between them and the ranch, Wes said, "We'll have to find us a tree with a good strong limb. We can't use the livery corral gate; the Rangers might not like it."

Travis said, "You're—not—?" His voice was a croak.

"We sure are," said Wes grimly. "You dirty rat, you planned John's death and waved that signal to Sam Sneed. And you stabbed Tom Harrigan, too, figurin' that the blame would fall on Bill. But Bill was too smart for you. Lord only knows how many others you've murdered. Bill passed his word that he'd let us take care of you, but he had to throw a bluff because he's a lawman and not supposed to condone lynchin'. And we aim to help him with his bluff. After you're good and dead from hangin' we'll fill your measly body with lead and report, very sadly, that you got shot tryin' to escape. I never thought I'd enjoy lynchin' a man, but hangin' lobos like Sam Sneed and you gives me the greatest kind of pleasure."

Back in the house, Bill was finishing his explanation. "Toward the end, Travis began to doubt that Malone would carry the election, so he fixed things so that he'd be certain to remain in control of the town no matter who won. He pushed himself foward in the Cleanup Party and got himself made its candidate. He had to stab Harrigan and he sure was puzzled when Tom's body was found in the alley behind the Frontier. I put it there, of course." He grinned down at Molly. "I just had to do that or you'd have been sure I'd killed him."

She said, "Bill!"

"Well, Sivart—or Travis—figured that if Monk was elected, well and good. If he was defeated, Travis himself would be in power. After his election he'd start the protection racket all over and he wouldn't care if he was caught at it, for after putting him in office the Cleanup Party could never hope to reform the town.

"He didn't bother about the councilmen. When one dies while in office the mayor appoints a successor to serve out his term. All he had to do was bump two of 'em off and put his own men in and he'd have a majority. Tonight Hollister and another of your councilmen were killed right off the bat. I imagine Smoke Rafferty did the killing.

"I didn't know at first how the roughs would take the election. If they knew that Sivart was the power behind the throne they'd have just sat tight and laughed; but I guess he didn't dare take the chance of broadcasting his plans and he'd already collected for their protection. It didn't matter how many of them were killed off; there'd be more to take their places."

Nancy came up to him and extended her hand. She smiled up at him as he gingerly held it. "God will bless you, Bill" she said. "I suppose your methods were justified, for as you once told me even our Lord used force at times."

"Thanks, Nancy. You helped a lot yourself. Not so much by what you did with the miners, for that was canceled out by Sivart's crookedness; but by helping me keep up my courage, by showing me that I had one friend I could count on to the end. I'll never forget you, Nancy." He released her hand and turned to Molly. "Let's go out on the gallery, Miss Reporter, and cook up a story for the *Clarion*. You'll be working for me now; I own it."

"You do not! We won the election!"

"How do you figure that? According to the latest information one of Malone's men was elected."

They went out on the dark gallery. They were alone. She said, "Bill, you always twist things around to suit you. You just won't admit when you're licked."

He laughed happily. "Oh, yes, I will! I'm licked right now, lady; licked to a frazzle. I'm going to give you that lifetime of service, bedmaking and dishwashing and all. I'll have to resign from the Rangers to do it, but never let it be said that a Borden welches on a bet."

She said rapturously, "Bill! Bill!" and flung her arms about him.

After a while he pushed her from him. "Hey! How about that ring! You still wearing it?"

"The engagement ring?" she said innocently. "Of course I'm wearing it. Why shouldn't I? Every once in a while I get sentimental and put it on. I love it. It was my mother's, you see."

He drew her to him again. "I see where we're going to have lots of fun tormenting each other through life."

He drew her to the edge of the gallery. Off toward Calder the sky still showed a tinge of red. He said, "The fire at the Devil's Doorstep is dying down and we won't be hearing that name any more. To me it's going to be the Gateway to Heaven, because I met you there."

THE END